Lung Chung
The Diplomacy of a Pekingese

Lung Chung
The Diplomacy of a Pekingese

Margaret Ironside

Ashford Press Publishing
Southampton
1989

First published in 1946 by Home & Van Thal

This edition published in 1989 by Ashford Press Publishing,
1 Church Road, Shedfield, Hampshire SO3 2HW

Although every effort has been made we have been unable
to trace the copyright owner for this title. We would
therefore welcome any information which would enable us
to do so.

All rights reserved. Except for use in review, no part of this
book may be reproduced or utilised in any form or by any
means electronic or mechanical, including photocopying,
recording or by any information storage and retrieval
system, without permission from the publisher.

British Library Cataloguing in Publication Data

Ironside, Margaret
  Lung Chung: the diplomacy of a
  Pekingese. (Ashford animal classics).
  I. Title
  823'.912[F]

  ISBN 1–85253–186–X

Illustrations by Ronald Ferns
Typeset in 10/13 pt Palatino by Input Typesetting Ltd, London
Printed by Hartnolls Ltd, Bodmin, Cornwall, England

Contents

List of the Chinese Characters

The Hero....................... Lung Chung (Prince of
    Royal Blood, literally Dragon's Seed)
His Father .... Kung (Duke)
His Mother .... Chu (Pearl)
His Brother..................... Fei Chiang-chuan
    (Flying General, a colloquial name for a champion)
His Beloved .... Kwei (Aristocrat)
His Girl Friend .... Charmante
His Elderly Friend .... Chink
His Beloved's Father .... Yin Yang (Water mark
    on a stamp)
Her Mother .... Pai Yün (White Cloud)
His Offspring
    Yin Yin (Silver seal. Signet)
    Hsiao Fu (Like his Father)
    Hwa Pei (Petal of a flower)
    Ling Ling (Agile)

Mandarin pronunciations are:

Lung Chung — Loong Choong, with the oo's a little
shorter than in English.
    Kung — Goong, with the oo's as above.
    Chu — Jew.
    Kwei — Gway.
    Fei Chiang-chuan — Fay jiang jewarn.
    Hsiao Fu — Shiaow fu.
    Hwa Pei — Hwar Pay.
    Pai Yün — Buy Young, with the ou as in French.

Introduction

By the 1940s, the Pekingese was the most popular of all the toy dogs in Britain, whilst in China, where it had once been so beloved of the Emperors, it was fast approaching extinction. For over a thousand years, the favourite 'Lion Dogs' accompanied their royal guardians everywhere, even on the last journey to the grave, and the souls of the dogs were believed to follow those of their masters.

The court painters recorded each royal dog on parchment scrolls, now treasured as the Imperial Book of Dogs, and the Empress Tzu Hsi (the 'Old Buddha') laid down a decree as to acceptable appearance and behaviour, including: 'Let its forelegs be bent, so that it shall not desire to wander far, or leave the Imperial precincts. Let it learn to bite the foreign devils instantly.'

The first Pekingese to reach Britain were brought from the Yuen Ming Yuan Pavillion when the Allied Troops sacked the Summer Palace in 1860, and the last of these five pets left behind in the hurried evacuation, appropriately named 'Looty', lived with Queen

Victoria until 1872. So you will see that we degrade the very royal Pekingese at our peril! Certainly, in this highly amusing tale of the subtle enslavement of various humans by their aristocratic companions, fools are not suffered gladly. The story is simple and sweet, related from the dogs' point of view, with a keen observation of just how idiotic we, their guardians, can be, if not kept in check, but without ever a suggestion from Lung Chung, or even the grumpy Chink, that they would want to live without us. The inter-canine dialogue is often hilarious — 'Do bark up — I'm a little deaf'.

In their comfortable, theatrical, and conveniently neighbouring households, the dogs have it made, until the apple cart is upset by Cupid's intrusion. Lung Chung, Chink and the coquettish, but fiercely loyal Pug, Charmante, hatch a plan to 're-organise' the marriage plans of Lung Chung's beautiful mistress, Claudia. The cliché 'he knows every word we say!' takes on a new significance — just supposing, as in the case of Lung Chung and his friends, he really *does*! How embarrassing! How stupid he must think we are! And yet still he loves us, despite ourselves.

Clive and Angela Russell-Taylor

CHAPTER ONE

'What a lovely puppy!'

'Oh, the darling! Look at his great eyes!'

'He is a beauty!' and occasionally, to the annoyance of the little Lion Dog, 'What a beauty *she* . . . is!'

Almost as humiliating as being mistaken for a German Dachshund, or a Prussian Pomeranian — a yapping, detestable lap-dog race, with no sporting instincts.

A far-away look in his dark, luminous eyes, Lung Chung wondered how much longer he would have to stay, like any ordinary puppy, on show before the common herd on the other side of the shop window, listening to blandishments which ceased to interest as the day wore on. Throughout the morning he had politely moved his feathery tail in acknowledgment of the unstinted chorus of admiration, but after a snack lunch he closed his eyes, and pretended to sleep. He

1

had caused a stir in the West End of London — no doubt about it — but after listening for hours to the same compliments, a fellow couldn't help feeling bored. He knew, indeed he had always known, that he was an exceptionally handsome white and cream Pekingese, for was he not a true Patrician of the East, a descendant of the original Palace breed, imported into England in 1860? Hadn't the kennel maids referred to him as His Royal Highness, Lung Chung, the most dignified puppy of the Imperial Race they had ever known? Had his breeder not declared that but for his unmistakable Dudley nose, he was as near to perfection as a Pekingese could be, resembling his famous sire, Champion Kung, more closely than Fei Chiang-chuan, his twin brother? Yet because Fei Chiang-chuan's nose was black as night, he was still in the kennels, being trained for the ring, while to-day he, Lung Chung, had been sold to the owner of this canine beauty parlour and dog shop — to be resold! Nobody — least of all Lung Chung himself — could understand why his nose had remained pink, but rumour had it there might be a blot in their 'scutcheon. The kennel women had hugged him at parting, and had kissed the feature that had caused so much to-do. They had earnestly assured him that although he could never be a champion, in their opinion it added to his charm, and Lung Chung, surveying his puckered wrinkled face for the first time in the mirror of the shop window, privately agreed with them.

But he had been astonished when Mr. Brown, his breeder, had suddenly come round to the same

2

opinion. Previously he had bitterly deplored the one flaw on an otherwise perfect face; but when he had that morning discussed the purchase price with the keeper of the shop, he had declared the peach-like colour would prove a distinct asset. The Public did not buy dogs to show; what they wanted was charm, and that air of good breeding and poise possessed so completely by the little Lion Dog. And were not Lung Chung's perfect points enhanced by the short Dudley nose, which was broad and flat, and entirely correct except in hue? The shopkeeper had answered that freaks of nature cut no ice with him — though as the beauty parlour was hot and very fuggy with scented soap (doubtless kept there for Pom clientele) Lung Chung had not been able to imagine what the man was getting at, except it was clear he did not mean to be complimentary.

Thereupon Mr. Brown launched upon a description of Lung Chung's good points. When you have taken the unusual colour of your nose so much to heart that you have seriously thought of asking the boot boy to apply some blacking to it, it is comforting to hear from your breeder's own lips that you have dark, alert eyes; drooping, heart-shaped ears feathered at the edges, which make a perfect frame to your noble counten-ance; that your full coat will be of superb texture; that your mane is thick; that you carry your flowing tail in a princely manner worthy of your name; that your short lion-like body is correctly proportioned; that your fearless air, and slight swinging roll to your walk, add distinction to your personality; and that you are, in fact, a Pekingese greatly to be desired by any person with knowledge of what is unimpeachable Pedigree stock.

At this Mr. Brown had paused, and taking a handkerchief from his pocket, had wiped his brow. A wild hope had come to Lung Chung that now he was to hear why, after all these months suddenly and miraculously, the colour of his Dudley nose was making a personal appeal to his breeder. But the look of gloom, which had been cast upon him, had shown this to be a vain hope; in reality Mr. Brown's opinion had not undergone the slightest modification, and that, in spite of all his beauty, Lung Chung had been, and still was, a bitter disappointment.

But the moment the agreement had been reached, and the breeder had gone away, the shopkeeper had shown himself in his true colours. He had winked at his partner, and, rubbing his hands together as though he were washing them, had said that although Brown hadn't believed a word he had uttered about the attraction of the little blighter's nose, undoubtedly it would prove a commercial asset, and draw the Public to the shop window like a magnet; that Lung Chung must immediately be put there, and not hide his pink nose under a bushel a second longer than was necessary.

These inconsistencies on the part of two human beings were puzzling and disillusioning to a small dog who had hitherto considered Man (which included Woman) to be altogether perfect. Thinking over the shopkeeper's perfidy, and cooped up in a wire cage, Lung Chung took a prejudice against the owners of

4

dog shops and beauty parlours, which lasted to the end of his life.

But with Oriental calm he knew this disagreeable day would pass, and felt sure that before dark, he would be in his rightful home. He did not envy Fei Chiang-chuan's orthodox black nose, for it meant that until he retired in his old age, he would be exhibited here, there, and everywhere; and being exhibited, even in a small way, was repugnant to Lung Chung, for he was a shy young dog, and very sensitive as became a Prince of Royal Blood. To-day's experience in the shop window had strengthened this outlook. Yet he was glad one member of the family was to keep up the reputation of the strain in the Show World.

Ever since he could remember, Lung Chung had longed to devote himself to one human being; to the King of England, or to the Queen, or, perhaps, to one of the young Princesses. Somebody he could love with the whole of his big heart. He now realised that his Dudley nose had removed all hope of serving the Royal Family of his adopted country, but he was sure there was one person in the world to whom he could dedicate his life. He sighed. He wished this person would soon come and claim him.

All Pekes' hearts are big, and Lung Chung's was exceptionally so, his brother had told him a few hours ago, when their respective noses had rubbed together for what was, perhaps, the last time. At the thought of Fei Chiang-chuan, tears gathered in the closed eyes of the little Lion Dog, and trickled down his wrinkles. He was glad he had managed to wish his brother the best of luck in the ring, and to express the conviction that not only would he be a champion once, but many, many times. What friends they had been; what games they had enjoyed, hiding bones and balls and biscuits from one another, and romping over the lawns with the other little boys and girls, and sometimes with the grown-up dogs. They had had the most terrific larks, and sometimes the kennel maids had joined in. How sweet they had been! These memories brought more tears into the eyes of Lung Chung; he was always a dog for the ladies.

Yes, he remembered, Fei Chiang-chuan had often warned him not to allow himself to be too sentimental, and on these occasions Lung Chung had stiffened his neck and stared at his brother, wondering if he would fight him, there and then. Ah, if he had known they would be parted, he would have taken it lying down.

'You see,' Fei Chiang-chuan had explained, 'you flop so, when humans come around, and squirm like a worm when they say the slightest thing to you, and fall on your back, and wave your paws at them. You're positively sloppy with the young kennel maids. You don't catch me making up to them, and we're the same age. And what do you get for it? A bone? A cake? No, not even a dog biscuit! They just say you're sweet, as if you were a lump of sugar. They don't insult me like that; they know better.'

'But then, you are the champion pup of the year.'

'That has nothing to do with it.'

'Well, however tender my feelings may be towards the darlings, I'll fight any dog, any day of the week!'

Lung Chung had boasted, 'an Alsatian, an Airedale, a Dalmatian! I'll take you on, now, if you like! Me, sloppy? How dare you?'

Fei Chiang-chuan had yawned openly in his face.

'I am merely giving you a word of advice. You're dreamy and unpractical, Lung Chung, and if you don't watch out, one day you'll give yourself, body and soul, to some human, and your life won't be worth living — from the time you get up in the morning until you go to bed at night, you will be at his — or her — beck and call.'

'But that is my dream,' Lung Chung had answered, 'I ask nothing more of life.'

While his mind had been wandering over the past, there had been sounds of yapping and snarling close at hand; and a dog had been dropped with scant ceremony into the empty cage on his right. After a few indignant barks there was silence, but the voice had sounded an elderly voice, rather like that of the oldest inhabitant of the kennels, but not so cultured. Lung Chung half opened his eyes, and peered into the mirror from which he could see the interior of the neighbouring cage. It was as he thought; a middle-aged Pekingese was now in occupation. He didn't look a pedigree dog; indeed, to call him a Pekingese was stretching a point: but you couldn't call him anything else. His coat, which had once been golden, showed distinct signs of the wear and tear the years bring; his ears were badly set; his body was long, and he had no waist, for he was fat; his mouth jutted out, showing a row of teeth; he could never have been good looking,

7

and in spite of his air of conceit, he could never have appeared in the least well bred. At the moment, with his shoulders hunched and a scowl on his face, he looked the picture of discontent. Queer how bad-tempered old people usually became; time seldom mellowed them; in the kennels everyone had had to give up biscuits, bones, and most of the special dishes to the old dogs, or have a quarrel with them. They grumbled and growled on the slightest provocation, and were frightfully greedy over their meals, gulping down their own at lightning speed and then making for other people's plates. This old man was probably the same — worse — judging by the look of him. Lung Chung firmly shut his eyes again, turned his back on the admiring crowds staring at him through the shop window, and went soundly to sleep.

He was roused from a delightful dream of a victorious battle against great odds in defence of a little girl Peke, by shrill barks. A voice at his elbow said:

'I am afraid, young feller, I've stolen most of your thunder this afternoon.'

CHAPTER TWO

Lung Chung stretched his legs, yawned, and opened his eyes. Immediately they met those of the old gentleman, who in the mirror was certainly examining his points with interest. Thank goodness the Dudley nose had been hidden between his paws.

'What do you mean?' he asked, remembering that a young dog should always be polite to his elders. 'You haven't stolen anything. I didn't bring a bone, or any of my toys with me.'

'No?'

'No, but I wish now that I'd brought my stuffed elephant, although the sawdust was coming out from his chest, where I used to bite him — in fun, you know. I was really very fond of him. What thunder are you referring to? Has there been a storm?'

'Ah!' chuckled the old chap, in a most superior way — enough to give any puppy an inferiority

9

complex for life — 'Ah! I thought you didn't move in theatrical circles.'

Lung Chung wrinkled his brow. He had often run round in circles with Fei Chiang-chuan and the others, but decided that theatrical circles must be a different kind. He could not bring himself to ask for another explanation; he hated to be thought stupid, although he knew he often was.

'May I know, sir,' he asked, 'your honourable name?'

'Certainly, my young friend. I can see you come from good kennels. As a rule I am very exclusive; it doesn't do to know just anyone.'

'Oh, doesn't it? Why not? I mean, what harm can it do — unless, of course, a dog has mange, or something catching?'

'When you are older you will understand social values, and why — apart from mange — it doesn't do to jump at strangers. You must understand my family is very old; the Oldberrys. Your parents will have heard of us. We date back thousands of years; at least eighteen hundred before the Christian era, and later my ancestors played a great part in the Chinese state ceremonials; only the most privileged persons of the Royal Court ever set eyes on us. I was named Chink, after my famous grandfather. He swept the board wherever he was shown; he had a most wonderful tail.'

Lung Chung had been well grounded in Chinese history by his illustrious father, and knew a thing or two about it, if ignorant, on the whole, of worldly affairs. Chink had inherited an ordinary name, and his tail was distinctly unimpressive.

'But surely,' observed His Highness, 'all well-bred members of our Imperial Race can be traced back for centuries.'

Chink moved his feet uneasily, and indulged in a good scratch before he answered:

'You have received quite a good education, Baby, even if you as yet know nothing of the theatre. We won't go into my family history any more. It's of no interest to anyone but myself; we recognise each other for what we are — thoroughbreds. So you have just left your kennels, have you?'

'Yes, sir. My father the Duke has been a champion twenty times, and my dear mother was Chu, a celebrated young beauty, and a pearl of great price, who died at the birth of me and my twin, Fei Chiang-chuan. Father can't get over her death. Our breeder says if he doesn't buck up soon, he'll be no good for the ring this year. My brother is a puppy champion and it is thought he will carry everything before him. I am sure I hope so, because I've been such a disappointment with my nose, you see.'

Fei Chiang-chuan had always said you must face up to the facts of life; not dodge them or pretend to be something you aren't, for if you managed to deceive yourself, you seldom took in anyone else. You became what humans called an escapist, which was another word for coward, and no self-respecting Pekingese was ever that. And anyway, thought Lung Chung,

11

Chink is much too long in the tooth, not to know what a pink nose means.

The old dog cleared his throat.

'I don't object to your nose, myself,' he said, quite kindly, 'and the ignorant crowd in the street outside seem to like it. You see, they don't know it isn't the thing, and few people will know, unless you tell them. Don't let it worry you; after all, we are all born with pink noses.'

'But the colour should change after ten days.'

'Well, you're not very old, it still may.'

'My breeder says it won't now that I'm nearly a year and a half. I look young for my age.'

'Yes, you seem very immature, but I shouldn't take your nose to heart, if I were you,' said Chink, condescendingly. 'Heaps of dogs, including myself, have absolutely no use for champions. No, the ring is not for me, nor am I for the ring.'

Lung Chung concealed a smile, keeping down his upper lip with difficulty. The old chap had to save his face. But perhaps he thought on these lines! If he did, it must be lovely to feel so sure of yourself, and to be as self-satisfied as ten pedigree dogs in one, when you had not a single good point. All that boasting about Chink's family couldn't be true.

'Thanks very much, but actually it doesn't often fuss me,' answered Lung Chung, 'my father explained it is character that matters. All the same, I suppose if you like the ring, it must be fun.'

'Pooh, it doesn't hold a candle to the theatre, where humans show off.'

'Do they really? Oh well, if that's so, it can't! I didn't know humans were shown for their points and training.'

'You don't know very much, do you? Of course, on the professional stage they have to be actors and actresses; I'll explain all about it one day. There's no dog knows more about it than I do, who says it as shouldn't. But I ought to know, for my mistress is Edna Williams, the most celebrated actress of the older school on the English stage. She's very lovely, and very clever.'

'Ah!' sighed Lung Chung, feeling all sloppy.

'Yes, we make a good pair when we go out together,' went on Chink serenely, 'I've just come from her dressing room, where I guard her clothes and possessions when she's on the stage. She has to manage without me at matinées once or twice a month, when I come here for my bath and beauty treatment. I bet the staff will be glad to find I'm out this afternoon.'

'Why?'

'Because when they come to her room and she isn't in it, I just make for them.'

'You mean you rush up and kiss them?'

'Bite them!'

'What?'

'Yes, I don't stand any nonsense! They know me by this time, and when she sends them to find things she's forgotten to take with her, they now come armed with towels. They open the door gingerly, and look in. Then they throw a towel over me and fly round

13

and out by the door, usually before I can extricate myself. Yet in the course of each week,' Chink showed his dentures, 'I get my teeth into at least one or two trouser legs.'

Lung Chung felt quite faint. He was learning more of the world in one afternoon than in the whole of his previous puppyhood. He nearly forgot himself so far as to bark 'You old beast,' but with great self-control, murmured instead:

'Surely, Honourable Sir, that is an anti-social act?'

Chink made a peculiar noise in his throat.

'Of all the sentimental pups!'

'Is sentimentality not a human virtue?'

'Sentiment is permissible; sentimentality is false — artificial — sentiment, not true feeling. Always, my boy, keep your commonsense, and do not let virtue run to excess.'

'No, sir. What a lot you know!'

'I have knowledge and personality and — er — family,' answered Chink, complacently. 'And now, tell me your name. You have only mentioned your brother's.'

'I am Lung Chung.'

'Indeed? A Prince of Royal Blood, literally Dragon's Seed? A grand name.' Chink paused. 'Your parent was surely in a somewhat high-falutin' mood when he named you?'

'It was at first thought I would excel my brother.'

'But the Duke thought no small beer of him, apparently?'

14

Lung Chung's knowledge of this kind of English was inadequate.

'I do not quite understand you. Perhaps you would kindly explain?'

'Well, your brother's name means a — a — (wait a minute, now what does it mean? I shall have to rub up my Chinese. Ah yes, I've got it!) It means Flying General, a colloquial name for a champion?'

'Yes, Honourable Sir, and as I have said, it was thought we would both be champions many times over.'

'Well, there's no harm in hoping,' said Chink, patronisingly.

The little Lion Dog summoned up all his courage.

'Mr. Chink, before we become real friends, I must know one thing,' he said, with adult determination.

'My family is every bit as old — older — than yours,' stated Chink, at once on the defensive.

'It has nothing to do with family trees. It is this. You admit you bite humans. Are you fond of your own mistress? Because I,' sighed Lung Chung, 'could not live without human society, or tolerate a disloyal dog.'

'Oh, if that's all I can set your mind at rest. I — er — love Edna; love her dearly. Better than any other animal.' Chink's eyes were bright with devotion. He looked slightly worried. 'Actually I am idiotic about her, and would die a dog's death for my mistress.'

'I am glad to know friendship is possible between us!'

'So am I, pup,' answered Chink, whose worried expression had cleared.

'Is she fond of you?'

'Fond of me! She thinks I'm the world's most beautiful canine.'

Lung Chung had heard that love is blind, and this seemed to be true, for nobody who knew anything about the Imperial Race could possibly consider that Chink was even moderately good-looking. If ever a Peke needed beauty treatments, it was he.

'I wish I could find an owner like that,' cried the little Lion Dog. 'How I would love her!'

Chink sneezed. 'Gosh, this foul scent; if they must fug out the place, why can't they scatter a few stale bones around? Well, to return to the subject of an owner for you; it's unlikely anyone would think as highly of you, as Edna does of me, besides, there couldn't be two most beautiful dogs. But you may improve when you're older; you're all arms and legs at present, aren't you?'

'I was a few months ago, but I thought I'd grown into my size?'

'I've seen worse pups. I tell you what, Lung Chung. My mistress is calling for me presently, with an author friend. I'll draw their attention to you. Oh, bother, I hear that girl Nancy coming for me . . . she always sets me by the ears. Do you hear the bath water? She never gets the right temperature, although I always complain. However, *il faut souffrir pour être beau*.'

'I suppose so,' agreed Lung Chung, who although he did not know French, jumped to the right answer.

'You are not likely to sell within the next hour, as you've been on show all day, anyway, I hope not.

16

I should like to meet you again, and establish our friendship.'

'I should, too, Sir. Would you mind telling me what your author friend is? Is it a man?'

At this moment Chink was lifted from his cage, rather roughly; not with the consideration Nancy had shown to Lung Chung.

'Come along, you nasty old man,' she said.

'A woman, silly,' Chink called out between his snarls, 'but there are always plenty of men round Miss Claudia Hope, judging by what I've seen.'

Lung Chung pretended not to have heard Nancy.

'Is she — very lovely?' he asked excitedly.

'Not a patch on my old Dutch,' yelped Chink, from the beauty parlour.

There was a sound of splashing water. His Highness put his head between his paws.

'Not a patch on my old Dutch!' What language! And listen to what Chink was now barking; just because he'd got a few soap suds in his mouth! Had he heard those dreadful words in theatrical circles? If so, they couldn't be very aristocratic.

And then, as he stared miserably over the heads of the crowd outside, Lung Chung's eyes met those of a most lovely lady. She was tall, and young, and fair. She had come! His Beloved! He sprang to his feet, and barked with delight, flinging his tail to and fro. She laughed, and waved her hand at him.

Lung Chung's heart melted within him. He rolled over on his back, and beat the air with his paws.

17

CHAPTER THREE

Claudia Hope's voice was very clear.

'The only one I am interested in is the little white and cream Pekingese in the window. Please let me see him.'

'The only one of all the dogs, she meant,' thought Lung Chung.

He stood up, his heart beating so loudly that it seemed to vibrate through the whole of his small quivering body. There were so many other puppies, and one or two golden Pekes, shut up in cages in the beauty parlour — all waiting for owners — and all (you might be sure) already showing off their best points. What a pity his Dudley nose was so conspicuous! She was interested only in him, but would she be, when she noticed that his nose was not the orthodox black?

'Look, Claudia!' said another voice. 'Here's a

perfectly divine cocker. Why not have him? He's dog cheap for what he is. Although, as you know, I adore Pekingese, and think there is nothing in the world like them, the price is exorbitant.'

Chink, by this time out of his bath, and apparently being brushed and combed, barked loudly. His mistress went on:

'You think not, Chink? You dislike cockers? Well, we must naturally study the wishes of your Highness (Oh, what a mistake, thought Lung Chung). I do know, pet, no dog can be compared to one of your Imperial and Ancient Race.'

Nancy said, quietly, 'Lung Chung is the best-tempered puppy I've ever handled. They are so often snappy and difficult when you take them in and out of these cages, but he is a dear. He's so beautiful, too, with his funny pushed-in face and thick white coat. I'll show him to you.'

The little Lion Dog was thrilled by this discrimination, and felt glad he had smiled at Nancy each time she had lifted him out and taken him into the parlour, showing her his little white tooth, which she had greatly admired. She lifted him out now, and he nestled shyly against her, then with an effort he resumed his habitual dignity, which he knew always knocked over human beings — though to think of knocking over his Beloved seemed almost blasphemy. Nancy put him down on the floor, and Lung Chung, concentrating on all his father had taught him about how to show off to advantage, put on his fearless air, and held his head high, in spite of his pink nose.

Yet beneath this courageous and dignified exterior, shyness swept over him, so that he could not look at her, although her scent was so harmonious he no longer noticed the fugginess of the shop.

'This is Mr. Lung Chung!' said Nancy.

'That's right. Put your best paw forward!' growled Chink, and then with a snap warned Nancy to go slow with the comb.

'Look at his charming little nose! How too sweet! How lovely his is! What a beautiful face and gentle expression!'

'He is certainly very unusual,' said Edna, 'undoubtedly intelligent, and I should say full of character. Look how he holds his tail!'

'He's just what I've always wanted,' sighed Claudia.

Lung Chung nearly collapsed with relief. His Dudley nose had not disillusioned her. She liked it! He raised his eyes. He was not mistaken. She was, indeed, even more lovely than he had thought at first sight, and she looked as good as she was beautiful. He decided that if she had been shown, she must have won all the championships in this country and the United States. Every point was perfect. She had large dark blue smiling eyes, set wide apart in a low white brow, a tender mouth that yet showed strength, soft, curly, fair hair, a complexion that owed nothing to make-up, while her nose, for her species, was unquestionably right in shape and hue. She wore no hat. The most cold-blooded dog in existence would wish for nothing better than to be her slave for life. The next second he was caught up in her arms, and Lung

Chung felt he had been transported to Heaven. He rested his head against her neck.

'I'll go into the other room, and bring his pedigree, Madam,' said the shopkeeper. 'I assure you he's worth more than I am asking. A dog with his points is worth at least double.'

'I'll have him; I don't care what he costs!' cried Claudia, recklessly.

At that Lung Chung shifted his position slightly, and put a feathered, delicate paw on her shoulder, in a slightly possessive fashion. He was hers. Nobody could separate them. Claudia had said she must have him, and so, of course, the matter was settled.

'Hush, leave it to me,' said the actress, in an undertone, 'I'll get the price reduced. I know Lung Chung is a real aristocrat; all the same, it is fifty times more than I paid for Chink.'

'Well, I never!' yapped Chink.

'I simply can't bargain about His Highness.'

'You can't bargain about anything; you've simply no money sense. Oh, hullo, Alan! And George, too. Claudia's buying this little Chinese gentleman.'

'Hullo, darling,' casually answered the good-looking Alan. But he greeted Claudia with more respect, and Lung Chung knew intuitively that both men had come to see his future mistress. You had merely to have eyes in your head to realise how both felt towards her. Although George was not quite so handsome, his eyes were kinder; Lung Chung hoped that Claudia preferred George to Alan, but he feared from the glance she gave him, that Alan was her favourite.

21

Fei Chiang-chuan had said he couldn't understand how it was that Lung Chung was always right about people in love. When everyone in the kennels declared that Champion Tom Tit wished to take Winsome Winny as his second wife, Lung Chung had said the great dog's heart was set on Jade, and time had shown it was so, for although the little girls and boys thrown by Jade were at first no bigger than mice, and their eyes were closed, and their noses were pink, the resemblance to Champion Tom Tit was obvious to all. Lung Chung's gift had descended from one of their ancestors, and it must have been useful in the days when Lion Dogs lived in the Imperial Palace of the Emperors of China, where intrigue was rampant. 'Because,' Fei Chiang-chuan had added, cynically, 'where women are, Lung Chung, there is trouble also.' Quite early in their joint puppyhood he had decided never to have any truck with the lady Pekingese, whatever the breeder might have to say on the subject.

'Surely you're not going to buy a toy dog, Claudia! If you want a dog, for heaven's sake have a real one. That terrier over there, for instance.'

Lung Chung stiffened, and darted his head forward to see more of this conceited puppy, Alan. Chink, emerging from his towels, barked sharply and showed his teeth. George laughed.

'You can't know anything about Pekingese, Alan. They are the pluckiest of little dogs, and were the symbol of the Chinese Emperors' courage for thousands of years; dynasty after dynasty fell, but they remained in the palace until China fell. My father had one that used to go ratting with the terriers, and was the most absolute neck-or-nothing little sportsman, always in at the death. He often killed rats off his own bat, and was never known to lower his feathery tail.'

'Thanks for the ancient history lesson. And I am quite aware you know a bit of Chinese, as you have lived in China. I don't like pet dogs, that's all.'

Claudia fondled Lung Chung.

'I can't understand how it is you can't see how lovely he is. But I expect you will, Alan, when you know him better. Nobody can withstand them.'

'Why don't you call him Pop-I?'

'Your eyes do protrude when you're annoyed. That's one up to Alan,' chuckled Chink.

'He's an extremely ill-bred dog,' retorted Lung Chung, 'and I don't like being laughed at, Mr. Chink. If I were not in Claudia's arms, I should turn my back on both of you.'

'Forget it. I apologize; and drop the Mister. As I consider your family is as good as mine, the formality is not required. Well, it is evident Claudia is determined to have you.'

'Yes.'

'We'll be seeing a lot of one another, as we are neighbours. I shall do all I can to make things pleasant for you. There is a girl pug — rather an impertinent baby, but not unattractive in her way. She belongs to George, here. They live on the opposite side of the road, so I'll introduce you, and show you how to get into her front garden. I don't know the small white and fawn lady Peke who belongs to your other neigh-

23

bours; they are away at the moment and I think she is being boarded out at a Guest House. In my opinion she is rather a snob, but you will be able to judge for yourself when her people return and the house is opened up again. I think Claudia knows them slightly.'

'Oh, thanks so much, Chink. I like little girls, particularly the ladies of our Imperial Race. Do you and Edna often call on Claudia?'

'In and out a great deal; sometimes I find it is decidedly inconvenient. Edna is so anxious to give Claudia good advice and to persuade her to settle on George, rather than Alan. I wish to goodness she would decide one way or the other, for until she does, there'll be no peace in either of our homes. Edna gets all worked up about Claudia, and even at the best of times temperamental isn't the word for her. She's an actress, and the more talented they are, the more difficult they are to cope with.'

'I like her very much,' said Lung Chung, dreamily.

Chink looked at him sharply.

'Don't you ever forget she belongs to me. I'll have more than one bone to pick with you, if you do. I have to remind Gerald constantly, and one person is enough. By the way, do bark up; I'm a little deaf.'

'Is Gerald another dog?'

'No, but he thinks he's a bit of a dog.'

'Oh, another human, then, in love with Claudia? They have good taste.'

'I'd stake my hidden store he's not in love with Claudia; merely a platonic friend. Oh, he's nothing;

just Edna's husband, and business manager; quite good at his job, I believe.'

'You have a Master, then! How lovely!'

'I have not. And bear this in mind, Lung Chung, if Alan or George marries Claudia, relegate her husband at once to Gerald's status; don't give him time to get the whip hand. Master, indeed! You're tellin' me!'

Chink's tone was so annoyed that Lung Chung immediately apologized for putting his paw in it. But, he added, if Claudia chose George, he'd adore having him for his Master.

'You'd have to share him with the lady pug I told you about, but if you want a master, I suppose George would fill the bill quite well.'

'He understands the Chinese and their Pekingese. Alan doesn't. He gave the show away completely just now. All men who know about us, respect our race.'

'Naturally,' yawned Chink. 'George is a fool to put his tail between his legs, and take a back seat whenever Alan turns up. He's just as gifted as an actor, Edna says.'

Meanwhile the humans had been talking to the shopkeeper, who was apparently not giving way to Edna. Claudia did not seem interested in the details of finance, and was more concerned in admiring Lung Chung, and showing his points to anyone who would listen. Alan had wandered away, and to show his superiority had stopped before the cage of an Alsatian. George stood by.

'You do like my choice, George, don't you?'

'Yes. Lung Chung's peach-coloured nose adds to his look of distinction.'

'Everyone agrees, sir!' said the shopkeeper, eagerly. 'And you will observe it is exceptionally short and flat.'

Alan turned round.

'I warn you, Claudia, he'll snore like a squadron of aeroplanes. I hope you won't have him to sleep in your bedroom.'

'Where he will sleep is my affair,' answered Claudia, with a touch of irritation in her voice.

Lung Chung smiled at Edna, George and Chink. He avoided looking at Alan. He was so rude that he was beneath contempt.

'Well, I hope you won't become his slave. You are the type of woman who does.'

Claudia laughed.

'I hope I shall never be a slave. And anyway, I hate to be considered a "type." '

Alan looked obstinate.

'According to George the little beasts gained complete power over the supreme rulers of China, and were exalted by the Emperors to dazzling heights. So look out! Besides, I'd be sorry if you lost interest in the play I'm helping you with, and of course —' he added, hastily, as Chink's mistress gave him a nasty look, '— other people as well are giving up their precious time.'

'Cut me out, Alan,' broke in Edna. 'Anyone in the profession could explain the technique to Claudia. She's an experienced writer, you know. As for dogs —

I personally have known a great many more interesting Pekingese than I have known interesting
people.'

'Indeed?' snapped Alan.

'You're both most helpful to me,' Claudia said
serenely. 'And so is George. I can't be sufficiently
grateful to you all.'

In spite of this generous observation Lung Chung
was certain that Alan, given canine teeth, would
dearly have liked to insert them into the flesh of both
Edna and George. He was sorry his mistress seemed
unaware that Alan was rather a cur.

Lung Chung's puppy exuberance had worn him
out, and although for a few minutes longer he fought
the feeling of sleepiness, he was eventually overcome,
and slept soundly in the security of his owner's arms.
He did not wake until he found himself in a new open
basket, in a strange room. A blue blanket covered him;
by his side was a rubber bone, a ball, and a teddy
bear. On the divan above was a small harness and
leash. His dear mistress had been extravagant; it
wouldn't have mattered if she had overlooked the
purchase of the leash.

'How do you like your new home, Lung Chung?'

Claudia was smiling down at him. His Highness
threw back his head, and smiled in return.

'Ideal,' he barked.

'I am so glad, little Lion Dog.'

There was telepathy between them. Lung Chung
knew that Lion Dog was a variation on the theme
of darling, sweetheart, beautiful, and other terms of

Home at last

endearment. His mistress would always understand him. He jumped out of his basket, on to the arm of the chair where she was sitting, and throwing himself upon her, gave her a licky kiss on her neck. He was glad Alan was not there, and that he had her, for this first evening, all to himself.

'Home at last,' he thought, and then hummed loudly: 'Heaven. I'm in Heaven.'

CHAPTER FOUR

Claudia lived alone with a maid in a small house in Hampstead. Mary had once been the mistress's nurse, she told Lung Chung, as she lifted him out of his basket the next morning, and rocked him in her arms.

'My new sweet baby. My 'ickle 'ickle darling.'

The Lion Dog closed his bright eyes, and, smiling, raised his upper lip to display his ingratiating tooth. That would complete Mary's subjugation. Not that His Highness exactly cared to be called a baby or 'ickle darling; for during the night he had made up his mind to grow up as quickly as possible, so that he could protect Claudia, her house, and all that was hers. Such endearments tend to undermine a growing dog's confidence in himself, but they are pleasant, and when Mary put him down, Lung Chung knew he had captured her heart for ever. She went into a room with lovely smells, and returned with a cloth she called a duster, and things she said were a dustpan and brush. It was the biggest brush Lung Chung had ever seen; it was at least three times the size of the ones used by the big dogs at the kennels to brush their coats. He at once stole the duster, and ran all over the ground floor with it, successfully dodging Mary until she gave up the chase. He thus learnt where the rooms were, and what they were called, and where the front door was and the back door, and the door that led into the garden. At length, panting, he laid the duster on a mat in the hall, and walked slowly towards the stair-case, gazing up passionately. SHE was there. Tenta-tively he put a paw on the lowest step, and waited to see what Mary would say. Dared he jump up, step by step, carefully? Would he tumble? He wasn't really a big dog yet, only pretending to be one. Mary made a dash for her duster, laughed, shook her head at him and said, 'No, not upstairs. The mistress will be down soon. You must now go into the garden, and do your duty, like a good dog.'

Lung Chung sighed, and Mary was at once brought to heel. She said very well, she would first go and see what she could find for him in the kitchen. While she was away, there were alarming bangs on the other side of the front door, and papers came hurtling through a hole in it, which gave His Highness a chance to show his mettle. He barked as loudly as any grown-up dog, the lid of the hole was lifted again, two eyes appeared and a man's voice said: 'I'm not frightened of you, little fellow.' He barked again, and the man ran down the steps and went away. Lung Chung felt proud, yet on her return Mary merely laughed at him and said he was a funny puppy. She couldn't have realised what had happened; she must be like Chink, a little deaf. He felt slightly annoyed at being thought humorous when he had been so brave, but his irritation vanished when he caught sight of the excellent marrow bone Mary was carrying. He thumped his plume on the floor by way of thanks, then stood up and waved it enthusiastically.

'Oh, you know what a bone is, do you?'

What a fool — even if a darling 'ickle one — she must think him. When Mary knew him better she would realise he was almost grown-up. She went towards the garden door and he followed her closely, licking his black lips in anticipation. Lung Chung's mouth was not yet fully developed, for he hadn't got all his second teeth, but instinctively he caught hold of the bone in the right place when it was held out to him and dragged it by stages to the bottom of the garden. There he put it down on the grass and sniffed it all over. Yes, decidedly it was one of the best bones he had ever had; there was plenty of marrow, and several bits of raw meat still adhered to it. He held it firmly with a delicate paw and began to gnaw. It was most succulent, and would help the last of his troublesome teeth to come through and complete his set. He must bury the bone safely before he went back to the house, for he knew it would not be allowed on the carpets.

He was getting down to it in earnest, when a bark on the other side of the fence disturbed him. He looked up, and to his surprise saw Chink looking through a slit in the fence, his goggly eyes on the treasure.

'Good gracious,' grunted Lung Chung, with mixed feelings. 'Do you live over there?' and remembering his manners, he reluctantly put down the bone, and added: 'Good morning to you, Honourable Sir.'

'Good morning, pup,' grinned Chink. 'I thought you would be surprised. Yes, these are Edna's grounds; in comparison, your garden is like a minute flea lost in a poodle's winter coat. That big house you can see through the trees is ours; all the same, there is one thing I envy that you possess.'

Out of the corners of his eyes Chink was still looking at the bone.

'Oh yeah?' said Lung Chung, evasively.

'Yes, your Mary. She's a positive old pet. You lick up to her . . . it'll be well worth your while. We've had a terror of a cook; she left yesterday, thanks to me; but I expect the one who's due tomorrow will be as bad, if not worse. I'm completely disillusioned about cooks. I see you already have a very decent bone. Did you pinch it?'

'It was given to me!'

'When you've finished with your present, you might shove it across.'

'I haven't . . . yet.'

'I didn't say you had, but you must learn not to be greedy, or I shall doubt if you are really accustomed to good Pekingese society. You've made one of your paws frightfully greasy. You'd better clean up before you go in to breakfast. It's your first morning, and you want to make a good impression. Where did you sleep?'

'Downstairs, in my new basket.'

Lung Chung, licking his paw now instead of the bone, felt very proud. What would the old man say to that?

'Oh, I sleep on Edna's bed. How's Claudia — merry and bright as usual?'

'I haven't seen her yet; I'm longing to.'

'What a dog you are for the ladies! Almost as bad as Mr. Alan Durrington.'

'Who's he?' asked Lung Chung. He was determined to keep his self-control, and not bark back insults. Retaliation would not alter Chink, for Mr. Brown had often said you couldn't teach old dogs new tricks.

'Don't you remember he was one of the lads who got on the track of Edna and Claudia in my beauty parlour yesterday. Memory is apparently not a strong point.'

'Oh, — him! I liked the one called George. I hope he is Claudia's favourite?'

'No. So Alan's scent didn't appeal to you? It is distinctly repulsive to me. Isn't he deplorably ignorant of the dog world, and of ancient China? Yet he's a big star in the theatre; the public's mad about him, especially the ladies.'

'A star? He looked like a man to me! Surely he is one?'

Chink was sufficiently Peke to stiffen his neck, and his eyes bulged more than ever with annoyance.

'I'm not going to answer silly questions like that,' he said, testily. 'You've seen him for yourself, and if we are to be friendly you'll have to pick up the technical terms of the profession. Oh, don't look worried,' he added more kindly, for Lung Chung had wondered where in shame he could hide his pink nose, 'you'll tumble to them, as your brain matures. I must say I'm glad you don't like Alan.'

His Highness shook his feathery ears right over his eyes.

'As far as I can hate a human, I hated him! I thought he was rude to my dearest Claudia, and he's so stuck-up. Surely he can't be a pedigree dog of any distinction?'

'He is a pretentious hound. Your mistress will commit a social blunder if she marries him. But unless I'm mistaken, Lung Chung, you and me are going to see a lot of him in the future . . . you, especially.'

Lung Chung's heart slumped.

'Surely she won't stoop to him?'

'It's almost a dead cert, and if she does, she'll be *his* dearest, not yours. Edna's more than upset about it.'

Some weeks ago Lung Chung had himself fallen in love with a lady at the kennels, old enough to be his mother. Fei Chiang-chuan and his father Kung had tried to laugh him out of his ecstasy, saying he was too young and she was too old, and that he must drop what was undoubtedly a mother complex. Mr. Brown had treated the matter seriously, and had parted them, and gradually Lung Chung had come to realise his elders had been right. Now who — who could part Alan from Claudia?

'You mean he loves her, and she returns it?'

Chink frowned.

'The beast is a philanderer, incapable of loving anyone for long, except himself.'

Lung Chung jumped to the meaning of the long word.

'He runs round other kennels as well as round ours, does he?'

'Always all over the place.'

'My ancestors! It's incredible he doesn't realise what a lucky dog he is, to be allowed the faintest scent of her.'

'He may have an idea at the moment, but it won't last. Already he's beginning to pay attention at rehearsals to a fluffy little piece of goods called Vivian who can't act for biscuits. Unluckily, Claudia doesn't realise what's happening, and when Edna hints there are rumours, she merely laughs, and says they are caused by jealousy.'

'But are you sure Edna isn't right? I was simply amazed at the way the bitches gossiped in the kennels.'

'That word, Lung Chung, is seldom used outside the dog world. Forget it. No, it isn't just gossip. I was lying under a chair the other day when they came off stage, and I heard what he whispered to Vivian, and I saw what he did.'

'What?' yapped Lung Chung.

'I can't tell you; it might put ideas into your head,

but Alan won't be true to Claudia, it simply isn't in him to be loyal to one person for long. So let's hope she finds out what a dirty dog he is, before the date of the wedding is fixed. They aren't officially engaged yet, but you don't want him for a master, or even as Claudia's husband.'

Lung Chung bristled. If he could ever bring himself to bite a human being, that human would certainly be Alan. And then what would Claudia say? She'd probably not have a word to throw to a dog, however devoted that dog might be to her. What a lot he was learning! He must face up to the facts of life, as his ancestors had done before him. But they had conquered the hearts of their conquerors, and had subsequently reduced them to slaves of the Imperial Race. Lung Chung decided that Alan was too bad a dog to remain in the neighbourhood, however reduced in social status.

'Women are blind idiots, aren't they?' grunted Chink.

'The darling's scent had led her astray, not her eyes,' answered Lung Chung. 'He's handsome enough.'

'Don't be so finicky, you make me dog-tired.'

'Sorry. Oh, who's that barking?'

'Your neighbour on the other side of the road, who wants to be introduced to you, but we don't want to be bothered by girls this morning.'

Lung Chung was not so sure, but clearly Chink was taken up with the thought of the exceptional bone His Highness had put on one side, before the conversation about Claudia and Alan had begun. Chink hoped it

37

was deserted, but at the bottom of his heart he must have known that he was indulging in wishful thinking. The Lion Dog, his head between his paws, noticed how his friend's eyes strayed in the direction of the delicacy. There was an excuse for Chink's lack of concentration on the problem that faced them; he was not Claudia's dog. Lung Chung heaved a deep sigh, and the puckers on both sides of his Dudley nose deepened.

'If you go on like this,' growled Chink, 'you'll be old before your time.'

'But what can I do? She mustn't marry that conceited puppy. We must prevent it.'

'Well, if you'll cheer up, I'll help you, if I get a dog's chance. Keep your ears pricked, your scent keen, and your eyes open. After all, I'm most successful in getting our cooks sacked, although, I admit, we go from bad to worse. There's your breakfast bell, you'd better not be late on your first morning. Pretend to be keen on punctuality, eveen if you don't intend to keep it up. You know the saying . . . "Give a dog a bad name"?'

'I'd say I do. It's not fair on us.'

'Life's not fair,' said Chink. 'Why should you have the luck to have Mary?'

Chink might just as well have said 'Why should you have that lovely bone?' Lung Chung went back to his own garden, and gave the bone a final sniff, for undoubtedly it would have to be sacrificed on the altar of Claudia. If Chink thought that in a cook shortage, he would be supplied with bones by his neighbour, he would surely make a dead set at Alan, and together they would run him to earth.

Lung Chung put his tongue round the hole left by the baby tooth he had inadvertently swallowed during the discussion; then seized the bone firmly and dragged it to the fence. Chink was standing up, smiling broadly, his tail wagging. One last look, and with an effort Lung Chung shoved it through the fence.

'Here you are!'

'Oh, thanks,' said the old fellow. 'Chin! Chin!'

CHAPTER FIVE

As Lung Chung ran indoors Claudia was coming downstairs. He barked a joyous good morning, then choosing the centre of the Persian rug in the hall, rolled over and beat the air with his paws. He knew only two tricks, but he was sure she hadn't seen this one which he had displayed in the shop window. Nor had she, for she and Mary stood spellbound in admiration.

'The intelligence of him! The brains of the little animal!'

'Darling!' cried Claudia.

His Highness jumped up and ran to her. She carried him into the study where the table was laid for breakfast, and showed him his own chair, drawn close beside hers. Mary explained that he must never jump on to the table, or steal things, at which Lung Chung heaved a deep sigh, and then smiled acceptance. He sincerely hoped the delicious scent of food would never lead him astray, and that if he gave way to temptation he would soon be forgiven. He had once gulped a quarter of a pound of butter off Mr. Brown's tea table, and the consequences had been unpleasant. As one of the kennel maids had said, he'd got to learn what was what in other people's houses. But even now, the thought of that butter made his mouth water, so that he was afraid he was not as repentant as he ought to be.

'I wonder what he is thinking about,' said Mary. 'I believe he knew what I said.'

'Of course he did,' Claudia answered. 'Now listen, my pet, this is your chair. To-day I shall have to leave you in Mary's care, and she has kindly promised to take you in the afternoon for a run on the heath, until then you will have to amuse yourself in the garden with your toys. I am sorry, but it can't be helped. You will be a good boy, won't you?'

Lung Chung threw a passionate glance, to show he would do anything his Claudia wished.

The morning was dull, for although Bill, the stuffed dog, did his best to be entertaining, he did lack life. At length Lung Chung dragged him into the sun, and using his body as a pillow, rolled over and went soundly to sleep, not waking until Mary called him in to lunch. She gave him a satisfactory meal of raw meat and green vegetables, and soon made preparations to go out. After she put on her hat and coat, she took the new blue harness and leash off a peg in the hall, which dimmed the Royal enthusiasm. He at once put on his most miserable expression, and pouting his black lips, begged Mary to desist, but she merely laughed and called him a funny little darling, if ever there was one. However, he noticed with satisfaction that the fastening, which attached the leash to the harness was of the scissor variety, which he knew he could nip open with his teeth, and so give Mary the slip. Fei Chiang-chuan, always so clever, had taught him the dodge; you sat down suddenly, so that the person who was leading you had to stop and the leash, no longer taut, came within range of your dentures. It was simple if you knew the trick; his second. What a pity he didn't know more! He would have to practise sitting up on his back legs; he'd quite got the idea.

So with Oriental calm, Lung Chung accepted the inevitable, and set off with Mary for what she called a run, but was in reality a walk. At first he kept his tail down just to show his detestation of his outdoor clothes. Certainly he was young, but why in this quiet place was he subjected to such an indignity? Did she think that he would run into the road, and throw himself under a car? Why couldn't she credit a Lion Dog with at least normal sense? He knew how to come to heel, and would always do so, when he chose.

Luckily the heath was not far away, and once on the grass Mary removed the instrument of torture. They went to the pond, where Lung Chung paddled happily, and then threw himself in for a swim. His legs struck out instinctively, and the motion was delightful, then, glancing back at Mary he saw with compunction that she was terrified. He would have to go back. He scrambled out, but instead of being thanked, he was again put on the leash and led away, and held kindly but firmly until the pond was out of sight.

'Don't be a naughty dog this time, or I shall not let you loose again!'

As Chink had said, life was not fair. Hadn't he gone back, when he could have stayed in the water? He pouted, disappointed at not being praised.

'There, run off with you, and get dry!' laughed Mary, refusing to take him seriously.

He at once forgave her. He had heard a kennel maid say it was a great responsibility looking after other people's dogs, and, of course, he was Claudia's dog. This thought made Lung Chung glow all over, so he obeyed without further demur, and got dry quickly. Several strangers came up and sniffed him all over, and a few of the more amiable chased him until whistled away by their owners. He then urged Mary to play with him, but she said that her puppy days were over long ago, and now she couldn't run because she had a bone in her leg. He barked back that that was no reason, for he had many bones in all four legs, but she sat down on a seat and opened a book by way of answer. There was nothing to do except to take the air, but the scents on the heath did not compare well with his home town. His Highness grew bored, and was ready for mischief, when Mary called to him that they must be getting back, and patted the seat beside her.

He put his lion head on one side, and looked at her out of the corner of one eye.

'Not me,' he thought, 'if I jump up there I'll be handy for the leash,' so he turned a deaf ear to Mary's coaxing and sauntered away until he found a hillock at a safe distance. He had a good view of London, where Claudia was, and he wondered if she were by any chance thinking of him.

A lady who was passing, smiled and said to Mary: 'We can't expect to be obeyed by one of the sacred dogs, can we?'

Lung Chung waved his plume at her in dignified acknowledgment, whereupon Mary suddenly pounced and overcame his passive resistance. He gave in without a murmur, and they walked soberly across the heath. Suddenly dog voices raised in dispute broke the silence, and Mary stood still to listen, slackening the leash. The next second His Highness had the fastening in his teeth, pinched it apart and was free. He darted towards what bid fair to be a good fight, and as he drew near to the scene of conflict, he saw two fully grown pug dogs confronting one another, snarling, while a little girl pug stood looking at them, undoubtedly egging them on. She was laughing light-heartedly. Lung Chung was shocked. She was pretty, and could not be more than six months old, far too young to be allowed to see a vulgar brawl on a London heath. He fearlessly pushed himself between the two combatants, barked first in one angry face and then in the other, and his masterly and effective tactics immediately separated them.

'Who on earth are you?' demanded one, as he stood back.

'Don't you see he's a white Pekingese?' said the second, nervously, for he recognised a superior breed, pugs being of Chinese origin, and, as a rule, decently educated.

'Are we living in a democratic age, or are we not?' growled the first, clearly wishing to continue the quarrel.

'How can you think of fighting in front of this young lady?' asked Lung Chung.

'It's a family feud,' the young lady announced, with an air of triumph.

'Um, not exactly,' contradicted the other pug. 'We're usually good friends, aren't we, brother? Charmante wanted to see which was the stronger dog, so that she could finally make up her mind. You see, Your Highness, she's kept us on tenterhooks for months, and . . . and we're both dog sick of being dangled. She must decide on one of us.'

'I have decided!'

The pugs turned in a state of great agitation.

'Me?' they yapped in chorus.

'I'll tell you within the next day or two,' laughed the naughty puppy.

The belligerents growled. Lung Chung noticed that Mary was drawing nearer.

'Well, do go away now,' he urged. 'She's given you her answer, and I won't have the little pet rushed into a decision she might regret. Clear off, do you hear?'

'Au revoir, sweethearts! See you soon, my lambs,' said the little pet, winking at Lung Chung.

The two dogs ran off together, still snarling at one another, but in a rather more friendly way.

'What plagues they are, simply won't give a girl any peace. I'm awfully impressed by the way you handled the situation, sir. You have great personality!'

Lung Chung felt very pleased. He wanted to lie down and roll on his back, but he felt this sophisticated young woman might despise such sincerity. He looked at her shyly.

'May I see you home? I suppose you've slipped your collar?'

'I slipped through the garden gate.'

'Same thing,' said the Prince of Royal Blood, in a grown-up, very male voice. He mustn't let this young thing put it over him, he must be almost a year older, and was after all, of a greatly superior race.

'I should be grateful if you would take me back,' went on the young thing. 'Indeed it would be charming if you would. What dreadful dogs those were, did you think . . . or didn't you?'

'All I thought was that you liked them,' answered Lung Chung, bluntly.

'How amusing you are! Do you know I see Mary on our heels? Hadn't we better skip off?'

'Oh, rather. Where do you live?'

'Opposite to you. I begged Mr. Chink to mention me to you, and since you arrived last night, I've been ever so excited! You're terribly handsome! A real dog!'

Mary, now within range, cried out:

'Goodness, if it isn't Mr. George's little Charming!'

'Charmante,' corrected the little girl, in what Lung

46

Chung sensed was a cultured French accent. Who was George? Another pug? Oh, of course; he was Charmante's master.

'I suppose I'll have to carry you, and lead Lung Chung,' panted Mary, as she bore down on them.

'By no means,' answered Charmante, who certainly had her wits about her. 'Come along, Sacred One!'

They turned tail, and ran like hares. Mary slowly but persistently dogged their footsteps, while they passed a delightful half-hour playing hide and seek all over the heath. But when they decided to go home, they managed to shake her off, for the poor old dear was completely winded. They walked soberly side by side, for both felt hungry, and were looking forward to tea.

'You're frightfully well educated, aren't you?' said Lung Chung. 'You finished abroad?'

'Yes. I haven't been long in this country. George managed to slip the quarantine laws; wrong of him, but convenient for me. They say the conditions of the detention are despicable, if you're a well brought-up dog.'

'Oh, yes,' agreed Lung Chung, vaguely. He knew nothing of the law, with the exception of licences. He thought how clever Charmante was, and how pretty, and how . . . unscrupulous. 'Is George one of the dogs who ran off just now?' he inquired, pretending he had forgotten to whom Charmante belonged.

Her puppy laugh fascinated Lung Chung. He paused, and hanging out his tongue, looked at her admiringly.

'George is my master,' Charmante giggled. 'He saw you in the beauty parlour, and last night he, too, told me all about you. That's why I barked across to Mr. Chink to give me an immediate introduction. I've been longing all the morning, as I've said before, to make your acquaintance.'

'Oh, *that* George!' grinned Lung Chung. 'I didn't — or did I? — tumble to it you were talking about my Claudia's friend.'

'You're tellin' me! Yes, he was her greatest friend until that dog-cheap Alan came nosing around. You'll have to push him off, Lung Chung, same as you did those pugs. There's no fun in George now. He's a changed man. I lead a dog's life in these days.'

'Poor fellow,' said Lung Chung, his heart aching for George.

'He won't play, and he's dreadfully quiet . . . hasn't a word to throw to a dog. By the way, he meant to buy a Peke to give to your Claudia, but through some misunderstanding he got me. When Alan turned up, he buried the idea of a present. Besides, he now thinks the world of me, as well as of Claudia. I fancy the comparison is not too sniffy. I'm Chinese. You know that?'

'Yes. How glad George must be to have you with him now!'

'He is. He appreciates the fact I'm exceptional.'

Charmante was quite pleased with herself, and indeed, she had reason to be. Such an accomplished modern young person! Such poise! They reached their respective front gates just as Mary turned the corner

48

of the road from the heath. Charmante's — or rather, George's — gate was ajar.

'I've been given heaps of toys — stuffed dogs and things,' said Lung Chung, hoping to detain the lady for a few final words. 'If George isn't much of a play-mate at the moment, would you like one or two? If so, perhaps some time when the gate is open, I could slip across?'

'I should, indeed,' answered Charmante, just like any other eager baby. 'I love stuffed toys — and balls! What can you spare? I'm usually at home in the mornings.'

'There's a Scottie almost as big as you are?'

'I hate the breed. Definitely, no.'

'A Teddy Bear, an elephant, a . . .'

'I'll have the Teddy.'

'Will you really?' said Lung Chung, quite overcome.

'Yes, thanks. Look, left of the gate; there's the hole big enough for you to slip through. Think you could come tonight, or tomorrow?'

'I'll try.'

'How is old Chink? I called out to him, but couldn't see him through the fences. Isn't he a frightful old snob? He's keen on etiquette and all that, but I don't believe his family's old, do you? He hasn't the air, has he? I believe one of his ancestors must have married a Japanese spaniel. Surely he's not true Pekingese?'

'Perhaps, but please don't hurt his feelings by ever referring to the Japs; he would be cut to the heart. And he thinks a lot of you, Charmante.'

'He's not alone in that, but it is rather flattering

when you consider what a confirmed bachelor he is, and how disagreeable to our sex as a rule.'

'His bark's worse than his bite.'

'I daresay. Bring Teddy at the first opportunity!'

Mary arrived, almost breathless with her exertions.

'Oh. Lung Chung, how could you? You gave me such a fright, and you, too, Charmante.'

'Nervous woman, isn't she?' grunted Charmante. 'Well so long, I'll be seeing you.'

She frisked away and Lung Chung ran to Mary, wriggling his body in the most conciliatory manner. It is easy to be penitent after you have had your fun.

'All right, all right, that'll do,' said Mary. 'All's well that ends well. But come along now. They'll be back in a minute, and I haven't even laid the tea.'

She spoke as though it were Lung Chung and Charmante who, with bones in their legs, had lagged behind.

His Highness sedately followed Mary in and out with the cups and saucers and plates of food, and then waited with her in the kitchen. It was almost an hour before Claudia, with Edna and Chink, came in to tea. Chink's shabby old tail looked depressed.

'A most tiresome rehearsal,' he growled. 'Alan's a frightful piece of work. And how have you got on?'

'Mary took me for a lovely walk on the heath. I slipped the leash several times and had quite a jolly afternoon.'

'Hate the place myself.'

'I'm afraid I'm an awful boy for liking things,' said Lung Chung.

'Meet anyone?'

'Several dogs said how d'ye do in a most friendly manner, and — oh, Chink, I've seen Charmante!'

'A nice little piece, isn't she?'

'She's more than that! And she's done me the honour of promising to accept my Teddy Bear.'

Chink smiled.

'I thought it wouldn't be long before she was accepting something. She's the kind that takes, like most women. So you've fallen for her, and now have no use for Claudia?'

'My rags and bones, no!' shouted Lung Chung. 'Claudia has my greatest love, and will always come first. She's human. But after humans, little girl dogs . . . ?'

'I don't agree; however, we won't fight about it. But you're a romantic youngster, and no mistake.'

'What are those dogs grunting about?' said Edna, irritably. 'Stop it, you two, you jar my nerves. Now look here, Claudia, Alan's insufferable! You must tell him where he gets off! There was no reason this afternoon to keep you hanging about for him. No reason, except he will gossip with the cast.'

'But he said he must speak to someone on business.'

'Business!' repeated Edna. 'Rubbish! Anyway, I can help you with the technique tonight. Ring him up and tell him he isn't indispensable.'

'But, Edna, I do feel it's good of him to help me, when he has time to spare!'

'Good of him, my foot,' said Edna.

51

'Men and women and pups in love sicken me,' grunted Chink.

Lung Chung wrinkled his brow, and sighed deeply.

'If only we could pull the wool off her eyes. If Claudia could see Alan as he is, she wouldn't care two sniffs about him.'

'I'll have to think out a way of getting seriously on his track,' said Chink, 'but it will be up to you to help!'

'But you know I'd willingly die a dog's death ten times over for Claudia!'

Chink said it would be more worth-while to live, and do something to solve the problem before them. Lung Chung went under the table, his tail between his legs. There he hid his Dudley nose between his paws, until Chink and Edna went away. Then he came out, laid his head on Claudia's feet, and gazed up in rapture.

'I believe you understand exactly how I feel, my dear little Lung Chung,' said Claudia, gently stroking his head.

CHAPTER SIX

The next month passed quickly for Lung Chung. Claudia, however busy she was, always had time for fun and a special game before tucking him up in bed and giving him his chocolate. There had been no chance to slip across the road and present Teddy to Charmante; she had waved to him once from an upstairs window, but that was all he had seen of her. Then one morning Mary bustled about with even more energy than usual, and when she opened the garden door, she told his Highness that she was 'off' for the day and so he would be going out with the mistress and her friend like a big dog.

Lung Chung skipped down the garden to the hole in the fence and peered through. As he expected, Chink was solemnly pacing up and down, stopping occasionally to pat his sides and generally inspect his figure. Lung Chung edged through the slit and ran up to his elderly friend, who stopped dead and stared in the most unpleasant way.

'Come for your bone?' he inquired. 'If so, I've lost it.'

'No, of course not! It was a present,' stammered his young Highness, feeling embarrassed.

'Then why have you come? I didn't invite you, did I?'

'No, Honourable Sir. I just thought we knew one another well enough for me to pop across. I didn't mean to offend you.' Lung Chung put down his tail and tears of disappointment hovered on his eyelids.

'I'm not offended. I'm busy, that's all.'

'Perhaps I had better go home?'

'Well, as you've come you may stay,' said Chink, ungraciously, 'but next time it would be better to stand on rather more ceremony.'

'I will,' promised His Highness. He noticed that his conventional neighbour looked worried, and was now sorry he had added to his trouble by jumping boundaries. 'I don't think you are looking well this morning, Chink.'

'I'm not. I have something on my mind.'

'I felt you had! Do tell me what is wrong, I might be able to help.'

'It's my middle-age spread.'

'Aren't you too young to have one?'

Chink looked pleased.

'I'm older than I look, Lung Chung, and I'm getting seriously alarmed about my size. I take this strenuous exercise every morning, but it doesn't seem to do a bit of good. I simply can't reduce.'

Lung Chung felt sympathetic. His neighbour couldn't help his tendency to run to fat; it was hard luck on him.

'What about going on a diet? I believe they are very beneficial.'

'You doubtless mean well, pup, but I'm not fond of criticism, however cleverly veiled. Actually, I've cut out all starches, but I can't get back my waistline. I no longer show my Lion form. However, there it is . . . the years take their toll, as you'll find out when you reach my age. And why are you looking so bright and gay this morning?'

Lung Chung had been feeling cheerful, but was less so now. He answered, almost timidly:

'I came to tell you I'm going out today with Claudia and I think with Edna.'

'I suppose, *I* am of no consequence?'

'Oh, Chink, are you coming too? How lovely!'

'There's nothing in it to make such a song and dance about.'

'Oh, but there is!' cried Lung Chung, forgetting he must not contradict his elders. 'I shall be with Claudia all day!'

'Stale news to me. I heard Edna order the car to stop at your house and pick you both up. I thought you'd come to tell me something of real importance.'

His Highness blinked puzzled eyes; he couldn't think of anything so important as being all day with his adored mistress.

'About Alan,' went on Chink.

'Oh, him! No, I haven't heard anything, except Mary has to get back in time to cook the dinner as he may be coming.'

'What's the menu?' asked Chink, licking his lips.

'Duck and green peas.'

'I might look in at the back door after dinner. I rather agree, Lung Chung, that we do, after all, know one another well enough for me to — er — pop across to you.'

'I'm so glad you feel that. The difficulty is I usually have my dinner in the dining room.'

'You won't if he comes, and I have the feeling that he will. Then, before you finish your meal, you'll be able to shove your plate near to the kitchen door, and when Mary goes back to the dining room, I'll nip in and finish your dinner for you.'

'I see,' said Lung Chung, with simulated enthusiasm.

'Tonight may be the crucial night. You might like to feel me near at hand. They were very friendly yesterday, and tonight he may propose.'

'Propose what?'

'Propose to marry her. And if he does, we'll have to put our noses together without delay.'

Lung Chung returned home feeling he had left his high spirits behind him. But after breakfast Mary took him into the garden and skilfully groomed him, as long ago on special occasions she had doubtless groomed Claudia. The attention and his breakfast of milk restored His Highness to his usual form, and when he joined Claudia in the hall he felt a much happier dog. She held the harness and leash in her left hand, but made no attempt to put them on.

'I'll try him without,' she said to Mary. 'The car's waiting. Come along, darling.'

They went out together, and a man in a grand uniform opened the door of the car. He must be a minor royalty at the very least. Lung Chung sniffed his heels, which smelt good, then jumped in. The man closed the door, got into the front seat, and they drove off in style. The Lion Dog hoped that Charmante had witnessed his triumphant departure without harness and leash. Edna sat with Chink on her lap, but Lung Chung took up a dignified position on his mistress's feet.

'Ugh, all brushed up and looking very doggy, aren't we?' smirked Chink, leaning forward. Apparently he had forgotten his worries, doubtless after too much breakfast.

'I'm glad you think I look smart. What's the name of the Kung who is driving us?'

'Don't you recognise him in uniform? He's not a duke; he's Gibson, our chauffeur. The other day he went across to your house with a note and mentioned he had seen you.'

'Oh, my mistake. His face seemed familiar,' said Lung Chung hastily. 'Chink . . . I've just caught the most lovely whiff through the window! Whatever can it be?'

'That's easy,' grunted Chink. 'Comes from the Canine Boarding Establishment we've just passed.'

'My bones and biscuits, does it?'

'A most exclusive and expensive place; all the PGs have long pedigrees. The girl Pekingese I told you about is there now, I have just been told.'

'Sounds — and smells — lovely!' Lung Chung lifted his Dudley nose and inhaled again. 'I say, could you take me to call on — er — the ladies?'

'I only know one or two by sight. What are you getting at? You're a bit young, you amorous pup! Or do you want to go sloppy over the woman who runs it? She's distinctly on the wrong side of forty, and has no pretensions to good looks. I'd have thought for the present that Claudia would be enough for you.'

Lung Chung looked pathetically at his friend.

'She is, in a way. But don't you realise I thought I got a whiff of ancient China?'

'Nothing wrong with your scent; apparently the colour of your nose is merely an external blemish. You are beginning young, I must say! Why, your own bone is scarcely formed!'

'Oh, indeed, I'm fully developed. Chink, do take me to call!'

'If you must go, go on your own! At my age I'm not out to be mixed up in love affairs, or to be chased by a pack of young ladies, which of course I should be. You'd better watch your step, Lung Chung. Popular as you are with Mary and Claudia, they wouldn't welcome female convoys in the front garden. I'm surprised at you, at your tender age.'

Lung Chung got up and scratched first one ear and then the other, to cover his confusion.

'Don't do that, darling,' said Claudia.

Edna drew away her skirt. 'Has he fleas?' she asked, anxiously. 'My skin is so sensitive to them. Yet, if one did not feel annoyed with them, one could not help admiring them! They are such vital and intelligent insects.'

'His Highness hasn't any,' laughed Claudia. 'Besides, dog fleas do not feed on humans.'

'I prefer not to give them the chance, for all that! Fleas delight in hopping on to me, if I'm anywhere in their neighbourhood.'

Lung Chung conveyed to Edna that her fears were groundless and the subject dropped, after she had very properly apologized for her base suspicion. To show His Highness she was sorry, she insisted upon the 'dear little gentleman' sitting by her side so that he could look out of the window. This did not exactly please Chink, but he made no audible protest.

They drove through Regent's Park, along Baker Street into Oxford Street and Park Lane, and then turned left towards Piccadilly Circus. Here there were constant stoppages, and the traffic crawled. At first Lung Chung was alarmed by the noise and by the huge red animals that throbbed in the taffic jams near to their car. Chink reassured him, adding unnecessarily that he had a lot to learn. They were not a species of elephant, or of any creature not hitherto encountered, but red buses which carried humans, and in which, when grown up, Lung Chung himself would probably be driven. Then to the surprise of the little Lion Dog, the car turned out of the streets he'd thought were 'posh' into queer, poor-looking, narrow thoroughfares and eventually stopped outside a public house. Lung Chung knew quite well what the house was, because the young man who had cleaned the outside kennels had gone constantly to the one in the village and had sometimes returned in a peculiar state, falling about and laughing most foolishly. Mr. Brown had remonstrated in no mild terms, and had said if Banks didn't look out he'd go utterly to the dogs, an unfair remark, Lung Chung had considered, for not one of the Imperial Race would ever behave with such utter loss of dignity; it was impossible to imagine even an ordinary self-respecting dog would so demean himself.

Why on earth were they preparing to get out? This was no place for Claudia.

'Here we are!' said Chink.

CHAPTER SEVEN

'But surely this is a pub!' exclaimed Lung Chung.

'How clever we are all at once!'

His Highness stiffened his neck and looked haughtily at Chink. His humour was feeble — as feeble as
the droop of his tail. You'd have thought, at Chink's
age, he'd have known how to swing it over his back
at the conclusion of what he thought was a joke.

Edna led the way up steep stairs carrying the old
dog under her arm like a heavy parcel, but Claudia
ran up with Lung Chung at her heels. The room they
entered was very big and bare, except for chairs and
tables. There were about twelve people in it, seated
round the room, with the exception of three, who
were apparently performing tricks in the centre for the
edification of the others, who were looking on with
interest. George was studying some papers, but Alan

was not there. Chink nodded in the direction of the performers.

'They are rehearsing. The chap who's whipping them up is Tommy, the producer, the elder girl is Vivian, the one Alan is casting sheep's eyes at, and the other one is called June. Silly things, sheep. I once chased some over Regent's Park, and got Edna into quite a spot of bother.'

Lung Chung was watching carefully, as tense as his mistress.

'Is Tommy a sort of trainer, or a sort of judge?'

'Sort of both,' answered Chink, 'that's why he's the most important man here at the moment, but when the show is put on Alan is the star turn.'

'How curious,' said Lung Chung. 'Tommy is not a patch on my Mr. Brown.'

'He's good enough in his way; humans have to be taught tricks differently from us. They're not so quick in the uptake as Pekingese, but there . . . you couldn't expect them to be. We learn almost everything there is to know before we're six months old, but a child of six *years* is almost entirely dependent on his nurse. They can't help it; as I've told you, their brains don't mature as rapidly as ours.'

'And does Tommy order Alan to do things in a certain way, and does Alan obey him? Of course, I know we Pekes are not obedient, except in the ring, or when we choose to obey, but that is different. Humans have been our slaves for so many centuries.'

'Alan snarls and kicks a bit, that's why there are all these fusses. He won't keep to the rule that the producer is always right, although actually, in my opinion, Tommy usually is. You'll soon get the hang of what they're up to. Claudia comes here to watch and gain experience for the play she's writing, and to get a sniff of Alan.'

Lung Chung watched silently for some time. Then he shifted his position and turned again to Chink.

'Are you sure Tommy hasn't had one over the eight? Because if he has had, I ought to take Claudia away.'

'My honourable ancestors, what makes you ask that?'

'I once saw a kennel lad in that condition,' answered Lung Chung, doggedly. 'Didn't you hear Tommy tell Vivian that the floor is a staircase and that those chairs are a pond? There's not a spot of water anywhere to justify such an assertion.'

Chink burst out laughing.

'That's a good one! I'll have to tell Edna when we get home this evening; she'll laugh herself sick. Don't you realise, baby, that until the sets are made and there are dress rehearsals, they have to pretend things aren't what they are?'

Lung Chung turned his back on Chink who, although not a true Pekingese, would understand this action of supreme contempt.

'You seem to me to be talking utter nonsense.'

'Sorry, little fellow,' said the old man instantly, 'I didn't mean to hurt your dignity, but it was funny; of course, to a young stranger like yourself they would appear — if I may quote from Shakespeare — to have

63

put an enemy into their mouths to steal away their brains.'

Lung Chung turned round at once, and with a short friendly purr indicated that Chink's apology was accepted.

'I know I'm not clever, but it is all so new to me.'

'Naturally,' agreed Chink, looking affectionately at his friend. 'I forgot for the moment. Oh, they are stopping now. I'll be able to hop across to Edna in a minute; doesn't do to distract the actors by crossing the room when they are saying their little pieces. They don't like competition.'

Lung Chung decided to stay where he was and looked up at Claudia. Her eyes were shining, she was clearly pleased with the show. For once she was unconscious of his ardent gaze.

'O.K.,' Tommy was saying, 'we'll stop here and take the beginning of Act II. Edna — that's better, isn't it? Or would you prefer to keep it as it was?'

'Much better — no comparison.'

Chink winked at Lung Chung.

'That's the bit there was a row about yesterday. You realise how even Tommy is a bit under Edna? So long — see you later.'

He trotted off and Lung Chung walked with dignity in Claudia's footsteps to the centre of the room, showing carefully his good points, but naturally unable to hide his Dudley nose. He fastened his eyes on the producer's face, and Tommy suddenly saw him.

'My word, what a little aristocrat!'

'You can pick him up; he's guaranteed not to bite people, but if insulted to fight any dog under the sun.'

Tommy lifted His Highness.

'You would, if provoked, wouldn't you, little fellow? I'd like to do the same at times . . . it must be grand to let fly.' He rubbed Lung Chung's cheeks, under his chin in a forward direction instead of stroking them in the usual way. Evidently Tommy knew a thing or two about the Imperial Race.

The sweet young girl called June joined in the homage, and most of the other people clustered round. The admiration was satisfactory, and not a word was said about the colour of his nose. How right Chink always was; they had not even noticed it! Suddenly Lung Chung saw the detestable Alan standing in the doorway, and the light from the sun falling on his face showed a mocking smile on his lips. Then he strode forward.

'Hullo, Claudia — hullo, everyone — rehearsal not started, I see. Good, I thought I was late.'

'You are,' said Tommy, handing Lung Chung to Claudia, 'we've had to take the staircase scene as June has to leave early. Edna and June definitely agree with me about it. But we'll take it again if you like. You can wait a bit longer, can't you, June?'

'Yes, Tommy.'

'I do like,' said Alan. 'We might begin at once, if you've finished messing about with dogs.'

The little Lion drew himself up and stiffened his neck, staring at Alan. In the background Chink barked.

'The pretty darlings,' said Edna, fondly, 'they seem to understand everything, don't they?'

CHAPTER EIGHT

If Lung Chung had not been carried off by Edna he
would have taken up a position in the centre of the
floor, and turned his back on Alan. But when he was
told to share a chair with Chink in the background,
he could not show the young man what he thought
of him without including Claudia and the others in
this expression of supreme contempt.

'My word, I'd like to bite the hound,' growled
Chink. 'Look at him now.'

Lung Chung watched carefully.

'He seems an absolute dog-in-the-manger. I don't
understand rehearsals, but I mean-ter-say . . .'

'Yes?' said Chink, encouragingly.

'I mean-ter-say — he won't let Tommy get on with
the job.'

Alan's loud voice cut short Chink's grunt of
agreement.

'The mechanics in this scene are all wrong! Claudia, do you realise the author has only allowed three people three minutes to change for dinner? Make a note to avoid that kind of thing. We'd better take the scene tomorrow, Tommy — by then you'll have time to have it altered. When I consented to act in this play, I thought at least . . .'

'I have the revised script here. If you'd turned up sooner you would have known it's O.K. now. Come back, you chaps, we'll run over it.'

'Tommy's good temper seems to be deserting him, and no wonder,' Chink muttered. 'I think I'll have forty winks. Wake me up if there's anything doing.'

'What Claudia can see in the cur, more than puzzles me,' said Lung Chung. 'I do wish we could give him the boot.'

Chink's answer was a loud snore. His Highness closed his eyes. He, too, would sleep and dream of bones and more bones, until Claudia decided to go back to Hampstead. Easier said than done. Alan's affected voice kept up an irritating accompaniment, and the hours dragged on wearily. George went downstairs and returned with a tray of snacks and cups of tea, some of the men went down but soon returned. June took the dogs on the leash for a short, unpleasant walk, and people grew more and more worked up, until Lung Chung thought actors and actresses lived (what humans wrongly called) dogs' lives. He knew of no dog who would willingly exchange a comparatively quiet life for the turmoil that was going on around them. What Claudia could see in it to help her was beyond his canine understanding. In the late afternoon Alan and Vivian sat down near to him.

'It's iniquitous for an actor of my standing to allow an inexperienced producer to dictate to me,' said Alan. 'You understand that, don't you?'

'Why, yes, darling,' Vivian answered softly, 'and it's ever so wonderful of you to have accepted the lead in such a poor play.'

'Do you know, I believe George is putting up a better show than I am?'

'Impossible! George can't act. In comparison with you he's a mere amateur. Besides, he's got quite a small part, except as your understudy.'

'Have a cigarette?'

'Thanks,' said Vivian. 'Oh, dash it!'

If Lung Chung had not been a little Chinese gentleman he would have said 'dash' too, when a lighted cigarette fell on his coat. He jumped up, quickly shook himself, and, with a delicate feathered paw, pushed it from the chair on to the floor. Vivian picked it up, and for a moment her eyes rested on the Lion Dog.

'An improvement on Edna's, I must say. If I liked lap dogs I'd quite like him, but as you say, Alan, give me a dog that *is* a dog! Oh, here comes Claudia, so bye-bye. I'll be seeing you?'

'Not tonight. Tomorrow, sometime.'

'Righto — *duty* calls, I suppose? Hullo, Claudia, take my chair, I'm going. So long, Alan.'

Alan had risen, and was standing in front of their

chair. Chink yawned, then stood up and winked at
Lung Chung. Quietly he inserted his teeth, and ripped
out a round of cloth from the seat of Alan's trousers.
The crime was so deftly perpetrated that Alan was
unaware of it.

'Come and sit down,' he said to Claudia.

'No, thanks.' The voice was so cold that Lung
Chung would not have recognised it, if he had not
been watching Claudia's sweet lips. 'I am leaving now,
Alan. I was rather expecting you to dinner tonight,
but . . .'

'But surely I may come? After all, Claudia, I must
put my professional reputation first. You know that!'

'I quite understand.'

'Don't be like this, dearest. I am the lead, you know.
Everything depends on me. And . . .' Alan smiled.
His condescension was maddening. 'I was — am —
in love with you.'

Claudia took Lung Chung in her arms, and pressed
her mouth against his neck. He felt her heart rapidly
beating. She did not answer. Alan went on:

'The part gives me opportunities. The playwright
saw me in it when he wrote it. Vivian realises my
difficulties here.'

'Indeed?'

Alan looked almost sadly at Claudia. His voice grew
tender, throbbing with self pity which, Lung Chung
realised, Claudia might mistake for tenderness.

'Dearest, don't be so . . . cold.'

'I'm not, but . . .'

'I may come to dinner, mayn't I? I'll see you to the car.'

'Edna will be pleased if you'll come with us.'

'Oh, splendid.'

Accompanied by Edna, they went towards the door, Chink and Lung Chung at their heels. When Alan turned his back, Chink, with a nudge and a chuckle, drew Lung Chung's attention to the smiles and titters of the cast.

'What a rage he'll be in when he finds out! He's always so perfectly groomed! Let's hope he'll show off in front of the ladies!'

'I do hope so! What a lark it is . . . the hole's just where it shows most.'

Edna turned her head, and noticed their merriment.

'Pekingese do make the queerest sounds when they laugh, don't they?' she said, and stopping, picked up Lung Chung and then Chink, tucking each respectively under an arm. 'Do you know, Alan, the angels really seem to be laughing at you?'

'Indeed?' said Alan, stiffly. 'And why should they select me as an object for their ridicule?'

'I don't know. Oh, yes, I do! The clever little pets! I shall never get used to the intelligence of the Imperial Race! How very funny! They have such a strong sense of humour. Turn round! However did you do it?'

'However did I do what?'

Edna caught hold of Alan. 'Look, Claudia!'

'At times you are maddeningly incoherent.' The gentleman was keeping his temper with difficulty.

'So sorry, darling, but those trousers are new ones,

71

aren't they? Of course, if by any chance it's Chink again — is it, Chink, you bad old dog? — it will be a lesson to you to be polite to him in future.'

'Whatever kind the Pekingese have, I must say you've an extremely weird sense of humour, Edna!' cried Alan, looking furiously angry. 'Do you mean to tell me . . .'

'I'm afraid so! A round hole in the seat, just where it shows. Most awkward! Chink precious, you did do it, didn't you?'

Chink lowered his crafty eyes.

'Isn't he too brainy for words? So much intelligence is almost sad in a dog! But I'm sorry he's ripped out the entire piece. I'll give you a new pair, even invisible menders couldn't mend it properly. When you go home tonight I'll get Gerald to lend you an overcoat. It does look odd, doesn't it, Claudia?'

'Well, it really does,' agreed Claudia.

'I can't see the damage, so I'll have to take your word for it that it's *very* funny! It's so easy in these days to get good clothes — makes it even more amusing! I tell you, Edna, everyone who knows you is about sick of that animal! A little poison in his water, and the world would be rid of a — er — dashed nuisance.'

Alan's good looks had vanished. His cheeks were flushed, and an ugly expression had replaced the customary look of self-satisfied complacency. His adoring public would not have recognised their idol. He sat opposite to the ladies, not showing off a single good point.

'He's in a regular pet, isn't he?' mumbled Chink, delightedly.

'I'm glad he doesn't suspect me,' said Lung Chung. 'I-mean-to-say, he's dining with us, and it might be awkward.'

'Don't forget to see that the kitchen door is left ajar, or about the place where you said you'd leave your plate for me to finish.'

'You're tellin' me,' yawned Lung Chung, safe in Edna's arm.

'Now then!' snapped Chink, 'if you talk like that, I won't help you any more.'

'Sorry.'

'I should say so! Well, after dinner, Lung Chung, join me in the garden, and we'll discuss future plans for getting rid of our dear friend opposite. If we give him enough rope, he'll hang himself. Claudia will probably get over this exhibition of bad temper, but if she sees him in a sufficient number of rages, she won't have him in her kennel, or I'm much mistaken.'

Lung Chung hoped sincerely that Chink was right. Alan and Claudia were now getting on well together, listening to Edna, who was recounting amusing stories of the theatrical circle, which bored Lung Chung because he did not understand them. Once Alan addressed Chink.

'Don't you look at me like that!'

Chink was smiling at Edna's last joke, showing his full row of teeth. When Alan was told it was a smile, he said he preferred the smile of the cat in 'Alice in Wonderland,' which made Chink show more teeth, for he grunted to Lung Chung that the story of Alice was his favourite bit of English literature, French books being, as a rule, more to his taste. When they arrived home, Lung Chung went with Mary into the kitchen.

'You stay with me, sweetheart, while he's about,' she said, as if she, too, disliked Alan.

Life had its compensations. The dinner that followed was quite the best the little Lion Dog had ever tasted, and Mary gave him a helping so generous that he was quite pleased to leave a goodly portion on his plate for Chink. The old fellow must have been peeping through the crack of the door, for immediately Mary departed to clear away the first course, he appeared. He went straight to the plate, without wasting a moment even to grunt, and in a few seconds every morsel had vanished. He licked his lips appreciatively.

'Any hope of another snack?'

'No, she said that was all, and when Mary says that she means it.'

'Pity,' sighed Chink. 'Well, come on out.'

They strolled round to the front garden, and stood for a moment beneath the dining-room window. Voices were heard in eager conversation, and once Claudia and Alan laughed happily together.

'Getting on well, don't you think?'

'Too well. I hope I didn't take all that trouble with his trousers for nothing. It cost me more than you thought.'

'What did it cost you?'

'One of my back teeth, and I haven't too many left, and it has made another very painful. Listen, I hear George's whistle! That means young Charmante must be outside in the road.'

'No, I'm here,' said a gay voice, 'I'm annoying my master horribly. He knows you've got Alan in there, so he won't come after me. I've been waiting here for ages. I do think you might have come before.'

'We'd have come, if we had known!' purred Lung Chung, earnestly.

'Speak for yourself,' grunted Chink. 'We dogs have business to discuss together, Charmante. I think you'd better be a good girl, and go back to George. Don't forget any stick is good enough to beat a dog with.'

'Is this the House of His Highness or yours?' barked Charmante.

Chink growled. Lung Chung pushed himself between Charmante and his old friend, and said quietly:

'I wish, my pet, you'd go back to George. I fear he may soon need all your womanly sympathy.'

'How do you know that's the kind of sympathy mine is?' snapped Charmante.

Lung Chung sighed. He was tired. It had been a long day, and his afternoon's sleep had not been sound.

'I don't know,' he said, 'but if you love your master, as you said you did, you will go back. There, he's calling you again!'

'But I've come for my Teddy Bear. Have you forgotten?'

'No, but I haven't had a chance to pay you a visit.'

'Oh, go and get it, Lung Chung,' put in Chink, 'we'll have no peace until you bring it out to her.'

'You won't quarrel?' asked the little Lion Dog, anxiously.

'Course not,' said Charmante. 'Hurry up! I don't want to keep George waiting for nothing. Sometimes he gets annoyed, and says he may have to begin to think of bringing me up in the right way.'

'Pity he hasn't done more than think,' remarked Chink.

However, as Charmante merely laughed at this, Lung Chung sprinted indoors. In the hall he heard Claudia and Alan talking to Mary, and his seventh sense told him the blow had fallen. Mary, too, looked excited, but not happy.

'Oh, here's the Lion Dog, Miss! He'll be — interested.'

'Come here, Lung Chung! After Mary, you must be the next to congratulate us!'

His Highness walked slowly up to them, his eyes searching the face of his mistress. She was looking radiantly happy, so happy, indeed, that it seemed almost infectious. If only it had been George, and not Alan!

Lung Chung knew what was expected of him. Anything — anything in the world — to please HER. He felt a frightful hypocrite, as with aching heart he rushed round the hall, barking with simulated delight, jumping on chairs, and tossing the rugs all over the place, in excited abandon. He leapt into Claudia's arms and kissed her briefly on the neck, before he sprang down again. But he could not bring himself to look at Alan.

'I told you he liked you!' cried Claudia. 'You're terribly pleased, darling, aren't you? Alan, you do adore his little pink nose, you can't help it, surely?'

'He's not bad . . . for a Peke,' said the condescending Alan.

On that His Highness sat down on the front door mat, and turned his back on Alan. He looked down into the dark garden, sadly. Claudia and Alan went back to the study. A chorus of shrill barks came from the garden; Lung Chung went out, his tail between his legs.

'Hullo, where have you been all this time?' asked Chink.

'Where's my Teddy?' cried Charmante.

'I don't know, and I don't care,' answered Lung Chung. 'Chink, all is over! Alan has proposed, and Claudia has promised to be his wife.'

'That's torn it! I must go to George at once. He needs me,' said Charmante, running off. 'Au revoir.'

'What a waste,' groaned Chink.

'Isn't it? She's absolutely thrown herself away on him.'

'I was thinking of my tooth.'

'Oh, Chink!' exclaimed the little Lion. 'How can she be so blind? Is there nothing we can do? Think of something! Pray do!'

'I may have an inspiration after a good night's sleep. You'd better go in to your basket now, and we'll meet tomorrow, and see if we can save the position at the last moment. Good-night!'

'Good-night!' sighed Lung Chung.

Until he heard Alan's taxi drive away, he stayed in the garden. The night air was refreshing, and the scent of the flowers helped to comfort him. After all, Chink was brainy, and young Charmante was on their side. Claudia and Alan were not married yet. There was still a hope, he thought, as Claudia tucked his blanket round him and left him with a gentle, 'Good-night, Lung Chung! Sleep well.'

CHAPTER NINE

After breakfast the next morning Edna and Chink were shown into the study by a gloomy Mary. Chink, with drooping tail, made no attempt to congratulate Claudia or even to appear moderately pleased, but his mistress put on an air of gaiety that more than made up for him. It would have deceived anyone not in the know, thought Lung Chung.

'Dearest, I am simply overwhelmed! I can't tell you how delighted I am!' cried Edna, clasping Claudia to her. 'When is the wedding to be, and where? You must have a good show! Now tell me all about it! I hope Alan realises what a fortunate man he is.'

Lung Chung looked inquiringly at Chink, who grunted beneath his breath that Edna had not changed her opinion but what, in the circumstances, could the poor woman do but make the best of a very bad job?

'We are terribly happy,' laughed Claudia, as she

was released from Edna's embrace. Her cheeks were flushed, her blue eyes were shining, and Lung Chung thought he had never seen her look more beautiful with that tremulous little smile on her lips.

'I'm sure you are! He's certainly a good looker, and when he likes has great charm. And he can act. Yet do you know, at one time I was sure it would be George?'

'Really?' Claudia seemed embarrassed. 'George? Oh no, that is . . .'

'He hasn't made a name, but he's younger than Alan, and he will. A delightful boy. There's no doubt of his talent. All he needs is a chance. If he is lucky he will be as well known, if not better known, than Alan in a year or two.'

'Indeed, I hope he will.' Claudia's blush had deepened.

'Oh well, as it isn't to be George, it's grand it is Alan,' went on Edna, serenely. 'You will be able to write plays for him, and will have a lot in common in spite of his dislike of small dogs. Now my old man can't act or write, but he's a first-rate gardener. I'd say, if we hadn't the garden in common, I might easily, in one of my moods, have murdered him years ago.'

'Sounds terrible! Do sit down, Edna, and take a cigarette. That's right, Chink, I notice you have appropriated the most comfortable chair.'

'The angel, so he has! Isn't he just too clever?' cried Edna, gazing in ecstasy at the complacent Chink sitting at ease. She took the next best chair and helped herself to a cigarette. 'I wished you smoked, Claudia;

I don't like helping myself every time I come in and for you merely to look on.'

'But you often bring me boxes to replenish my supplies. Is it true that the Everards are coming back in a month or two and opening up their house?'

'I believe so.' Edna blew several smoke rings into the air. 'You know them slightly? We don't; they're a bit exclusive, like their lady Peke. When you're married, Claudia, I expect you'll take to smoking. It's a wonderful help as a husband soother. What date is the wedding? I suppose Alan has telephoned to say there's been a hitch and that we're to go on tour before the play comes on in London?'

'Yes, we shall wait until the first night here is well over; nothing must interfere with Alan's career, of course.'

'Of course, nothing must interfere with that,' agreed Edna, with a flicker of the eyelids.

'You hear what people say; you can't hear what they think,' mused Lung Chung, 'but I believe I can read Edna's mind correctly.'

'Yes, everything depends on the length of the tour. You know, Edna, I'm sorry about George. I hope he won't be very cut up. I am as fond of him as I would be of a brother.'

'Possibly, but you may take it from me, my dear, George doesn't want any more sisters.'

'The play is to come on at the Winalot, I believe.'
Edna nodded.

His Highness looked at Chink.

'Why have they switched the discussion on to dog

biscuits? Of course, it's easy to see Claudia isn't happy about George.'

'My ancestors!' ejaculated Chink. 'Winalot is the name of a well-known London theatre. How ignorant you are, Lung Chung! Well, it's satisfactory to know that we've a good many weeks ahead before the marriage. We ought to be able to stop it and get Alan the sack. He bores me stiff.'

Lung Chung refrained from uttering his opinion that Chink was in any case a bit stiff in the limbs. Edna held out a letter.

'By the way, Claudia, Gerald asked me to give you this note of congratulation. I expect he'll look you up this evening.'

'Thanks so much. Won't you both come in to dinner? And Chink, too, of course.'

Chink wagged his tail and Lung Chung thumped his on the edge of his basket when Edna accepted the invitation.

'What expressive eyes! Yet the little Lion looks rather sad this morning, or am I imagining it? Come along, Chink, we simply must go; I've oceans to do before we go to the rehearsal. Once more, Claudia darling, I must tell you how very, very glad I am.'

'Trust Edna to make a bally-hoo on the slightest provocation,' muttered Chink. 'I can tell you, Lung Chung, although time is not as important a factor as it threatened to be, it isn't going to be as easy to nip this romance in the bud as it was to nip that piece of cloth out of Alan's trousers.'

'Oh, if only she weren't barking up the wrong tree!'

signed His Highness. 'It makes me feel very temperamental.'

'Don't you start,' answered Chink. 'I didn't get a wink of sleep myself last night, and I warn you my temper isn't as good as it usually is.'

'No? All the same, Chink, just listen to this before you go. I've had an idea this morning.'

'Bark it up then, for goodness' sake.'

'It may not be any use.'

'I don't suppose it is, but as I'm here I may as well hear it. Out of mouths of babes and sucklings . . . you doubtless know the quotation?'

'I am afraid I don't.'

'You can ask someone else what it means then,' snapped Chink. 'But make no bones about it, Lung Chung, if we are to shake off this fellow, we shall need all your teeth. Mine are not what they used to be.'

'I hope not all!' cried Lung Chung. 'The idea I've got hasn't anything to do with teeth.'

'O.K., you may drop the bone of contention, but I do hate selfishness. What is your plan?'

'I just thought that the next time I'm taken to a rehearsal I could insert myself between Alan's feet and trip him up when he's showing off his best points.'

'Um, not too bad. You realise he is the type of man who wouldn't scruple to kick a dog?'

'What are a few kicks in such a cause?'

'They can be painful when you have chronic lumbago.'

'But I haven't.'

'Don't flaunt your youth at me! We were all young once, and the day will come when you're my age. I only hope you'll be as good a specimen!'

'Oh, I do hope so too! I didn't mean to flaunt.'

'That's just as well, for there's life in the old dog yet, my pup! Now let me think; yes, it's not a bad idea.'

Chink sat down on the garden path and Lung Chung stood by in a state of great suspense.

'Got it!' cried Chink, his wrinkled brow clearing.

'Oh, what?'

'It will want a lot of doing, but I think you're dog enough.'

'Go on! Go on!' barked Lung Chung.

'Watch me.'

Slowly, uttering a faint whine, Chink rolled over on his side and lay gasping for breath. Then, creaking with rheumatism, he rose, shook himself, and smiled with his full row of teeth. Lung Chung was quivering with excitement.

'See?'

'I see, but what's at the back of it?'

'Do you know what a veterinary surgeon is?'

'We had one at the kennels. My breeder said, though, he had no use for any of them . . . that he'd as soon consult a good fortune teller.'

'Mr. Brown is a man of sound sense. It's the one subject on which I don't see eye to eye with Edna — when she imagines I have a headache or even look pale, she telephones to William Berry, the celebrated Peke heart specialist. The fee for one visit would keep me in bones for a year. I know our great Race is rather subject to cardiac weakness, but although I'm not as young as I was my heart is still as sound as a bell — yet whenever he comes I am made to swallow filthy pills, and he sticks a needle into me which he calls giving me an injection.'

'How horrible!'

'Um, yes.' Then Chink winked slowly with his left eye. 'All the same, I've managed to get in several nasty nips. He's not as keen on calling as he used to be, but he'll be quite glad to get a new patient in you.'

'But I'm not ill! I'm well over all my puppy troubles, my teeth are now complete, and it won't be long before I get my full coat.'

'Oh yeah, but what's wrong with your having an enlarged heart? Actually, with your adoration of humans, you may well have one. Now listen, after Alan's kicked you, good and proper, you must groan and fall over, same as I did just now; realistically, mind. When Mr. Berry comes along, you'll have to pretend to be on the point of death. He'll be only too glad to be taken in, for he has an obsession that every Pekingese has heart weakness, and he finds it whether it's there or not.'

'But I don't want a needle jabbed into me, I've a sensitive skin. Oh, very well, I will if it's really necessary. But where is this getting us? Wouldn't it be better if Alan kicked you? You're a much better actor — that roll over just now was convincing!'

'I trust I've picked up a few tips from the profession,' said Chink, grumpily, 'but don't you realise Claudia wouldn't care a mutton bone if he kicked me? But if Alan hurt her darling 'ickle 'ickle . . .'

Lung Chung drew himself up, then softened.

'Please don't laugh at me. Chink, it certainly is a brainwave! If I acted the part well enough, do you really think it might crack up the marriage? Would Claudia mind as much as that?'

'Just roll over and let me see if you have artistic talent. Do exactly as I did.'

Lung Chung obeyed, then got up and regarded Chink anxiously.

'Not bad, but you want a bit of rehearsing. We can try it out this evening and every morning before breakfast, when I don't oversleep. After a month or so you should be perfect in the part. Ah, Edna's going at last! I can't say I'm sorry. I want my lunch, I'm dog tired after all this brain work. Put on your most innocent expression, baby, they are looking round and they mustn't suspect us of any funny business. Edna's not yet paid for Alan's new pants.'

Lung Chung felt the hour had struck to show his new trick. He sat up on his back legs and stayed there with perfect balance while the humans stood entranced. Then he lifted his upper lip and showed his little white tooth.

'I do wish Chink could smile like that!' cried Edna, enthusiastically. 'It's cherubic! My sweet will insist on showing the whole of his upper row, and people think he means to bite them. I'm afraid his mouth isn't his best point.'

Chink scowled at Lung Chung, who lowered himself with dignity and apologized:

'You practically told me to!'

'I didn't tell you to sop up to Edna,' growled Chink. 'She's my property, I've told you before, and don't you forget it.'

Claudia hastily picked up Lung Chung.

'Oh, Chink wouldn't hurt him,' laughed Edna. 'He'd never fight a dog younger than himself, I will say that for him! Pekes always make those queer noises when they talk to one another.'

'But look at his mouth!'

'He can't help showing his dear pearly-wirlies, can you, dear one?'

Chink smiled more broadly as he looked at His Highness nestling in Claudia's arms.

'What fools these mortals be!'

'Oh no, I simply can't agree with you,' barked Lung Chung, loyally.

CHAPTER TEN

That evening George Weston, Charmante's master, called to offer congratulations. His Highness, alone in the drawing room, welcomed the young man, at first with becoming dignity, and then with growing enthusiasm. George was tall, and while he waited, seated on a low chair, he stretched out his legs on the floor. Lung Chung darted forward and ran straight up them, burying his head under George's chin. He simply had to express his sympathy. The young man was so sweet, and looked — when he thought he was alone — so unhappy.

George laughed and stroked the head of the Lion Dog.

'You seem sorry for me, little fellow. Charmante, too, is most sympathetic! "The more I see of men, the more I love my dog." '

Claudia came in, and George, putting Lung Chung gently on the floor, stood up.

'I must apologize for coming so early.'

'No! No! I'm so glad to see you. You must stay to dinner; Edna and Gerald are coming.'

'Thanks so much, but I can't manage it tonight. You do know how I wish you and Alan all happiness?'

'Yes, I know,' answered Claudia, nervously.

Lung Chung crossed to the door. It was a case of two's company, three's none; besides, Chink was expecting him. And there, by the gap in the fence, stood the old man, shuffling his feet.

'I don't like to be kept waiting.'

'Sorry. But someone had to welcome George. He looked in to offer congratulations, poor fellow.'

'You do take yourself seriously, don't you? Well, are you ready? I wish I could squeeze through into your domain, but the slimming salts haven't done much good so far.'

'Then you'd like me to come through to you?'

'Yes, don't catch your new coat on that rusty nail.'

Lung Chung jumped through without mishap. He looked round.

'I suppose you don't feel like a game of hide and seek, do you? Too many bones in your legs?'

'Too much lumber in my lumbar regions. I've toothache as well. It puts me off my grub. By the way, you've just missed Charmante. She'd have been glad to stretch her legs.'

'Oh dear!'

'I told her we were meeting on business and sent

her off. She mentioned if you don't take Teddy across to her soon, she'll never speak to you again. Have you been studying your script?'

Lung Chung scratched an ear to give himself time for thought. He did not wish to lose face.

'Script!' he hesitated.

'Your part, then. Have you tried the roll-over turn again?'

'Yes, I think I'm getting on fairly well.'

'Show me.'

Lung Chung groaned loudly, rolled over and lay panting, his red tongue out, his eyes shut.

'Do it again.'

The order was obeyed.

'Not bad for an amateur; you may be some good later on. Don't close your eyes; stare ahead with a look of intense agony.'

'It seems frightfully deceitful.'

'Now look here,' said Chink, 'if you're going to have scruples every two seconds, I won't produce you. This is nothing to what you'll have to do before you see the job through. I'd be sorry if Claudia marries a man like Alan, and more sorry for you with him for a master, but if you keep raising objections like this I'll lose interest.'

'I promise I won't again!' and Lung Chung stared ahead in agony that was partly real. It would be impossible to tackle this affair without Chink's help and vast experience.

'Yes, that'll do. Quite promising. I'll make an actor of you yet, though you'll never be first class. But you

are word perfect, artistic feeling is what you lack —
realism, my pup! But you will probably acquire it after
you've had a good hard kick. Would you like a stroll
round the grounds? We have some good lilac this year;
Edna means to wear a piece tonight. I can't spare you
long, as I shall have to tog myself up a bit before I
join her and Gerald. Don't worry, Lung Chung, I'll
see to it that we cover our tracks after you've played
your part in a way to do me credit.'

They inspected the spring flowers, and Chink
allowed His Highness to play with some fallen
laburnum petals which were blowing about in the
wind.

'Ah,' he said, sentimentally, 'if I had a daughter, I
should call her Petal.'

'Don't be a fool,' scoffed Chink. 'Au revoir now! I'll
be seein' you.'

The little Lion Dog skipped back to the fence; there
were exhilarating scents in the air! He sniffed them
with delight, and then, becoming more practical, he
looked round to see if his bones were safely concealed
and carefully buried them again, before he went home
in excellent spirits. He had said his little piece, he had
won praise from Chink, and the unusual scents in the
air caused him new and exquisite pleasure. He must
ask Chink what they were. Once indoors he walked
into the drawing room with grown up confidence in
himself, his tail flung high in a great curve over his
back, his head well up. George had left, but the odious
Alan, with Edna and Gerald, was there, and Alan,
smiling like Chink, was showing all his teeth. Claudia

at once noticed her Lion Dog and put out a small foot in a satin shoe to be guarded. As he lay across it there was a chorus of admiration and Edna, obviously to annoy Alan, told many stories of the Imperial Race, which illustrated the courage, loyalty, resource, sense of humour, and sportsmanship of the Pekingese, ancient and modern, and of their venerable ancestors. Lung Chung listened with pride, and for the first time heard the legend of his origin; how the Lion with the great heart fell in love with a tiny and lovely lady monkey. The lady did not like his size, so he begged the Lord Buddha to reduce it, but to keep his Lion Heart intact, so that he could continue to love as ardently as before. His request (because he so greatly loved) was granted, and his size was changed, leaving him his courage, his Lion form, and a greater heart than that of any other living creature.

This story was naturally extremely gratifying to His Highness and made him again think of the scents outside and of Charmante. Was he prepared to become pug for her sake? Was he willing to have children who, however sweet they might be, would undoubtedly be pug-peke? He thought not; the idea of Charmante as a young sister, to whom he could recount his love affairs, was more agreeable.

'You talk, Edna,' commented Alan in affected disgust, 'as though the Pekingese were human beings.'

'They are, almost. They have been highly civilised for thousands of years, long before we were. They had human foster-mothers as well as their own retainers.

That is why they will only obey when they feel inclined. And haven't you noticed they don't whine, but cry like children?'

Chink walked into the room, and Lung Chung was sure he had been listening at the door, for he was looking more than usually stuck up.

'I'd like to have the chance of hearing them cry, but there isn't any chance when they are all so pampered.'

Lung Chung stiffened and darted forward his head to try and wither Alan with a look. Edna and her husband changed the subject and once more congratulated Alan. All the humans were bemoaning the fact that as the play was not coming on in London at once, but going to the provinces instead, there would be no more rehearsals for the present. Lung Chung was glad Claudia would have more time to play with him, as she was staying in London. At this point Chink winked at him, jumped forward, and nipped Alan's elegant ankles. The young man gave a startled cry. Edna laughed:

'That's to show you that the Pekingese — like the elephants — never forget. You should be careful to see where Chink is, Alan, for I shall not pay for a second pair. Come here, precious, don't let the naughty man touch you!'

Chink, who had shown no intention of allowing Alan to come near him, ran to Edna, who caught him up and kissed him.

'You see,' he barked, 'how easy it is, don't you? It's your turn now, Lung Chung.'

'But I couldn't possibly bite him, even if I hated him

ten times more than I do! I was brought up never to bite any human. Honestly, Chink, it's not done in the best Pekingese circles, even if it is in theatrical ones!'

'If you don't soon jolly well pull your weight, I'll walk out on our two months' plan,' snarled Chink.

Lung Chung's wrinkles deepened. He was worried. He simply couldn't bite, and he couldn't think of anything else that could be done until the rehearsals began again. If only Alan were an Alsatian, an Airedale, a big dog of any sort, he'd soon show Chink what he was made of. He got up and went into the hall. Perhaps the cool delicious spring air would bring inspiration. The front door stood open, and there, framed in the doorway, stood Mademoiselle Charmante. His Highness, who would have enthusiastically welcomed her at any other moment, felt perturbed. He had left the party so that he could think things over, but what dog could think seriously with this fascinating little girl looking at him with her great pug eyes?

'Oh, hullo!' he said, awkwardly.

'You don't look a bit pleased to see me!'

'But I am! Of course! I mean, who wouldn't be?' wriggled Lung Chung.

'Methinks you do protest too much.'

'What's that? Oh no, indeed, I am delighted to see you. Why, I was only thinking about you a few minutes ago!'

'What were you thinking?'

Pug-pekes? No, he couldn't mention them, or of his

idea of leaving the Royal Race to become just pug himself. So he answered evasively:

'A beautiful little monkey was mentioned. She — somehow — made me think of you.'

'I'm not flattered. Is George in there?'

'No, darling. He must have left some time ago. I believe he said he'd look up a friend at the B.B.C. Have you heard the play's going on tour? What are they going to do with you?'

'Oh, the usual. The housekeeper looks after me. I like being with George, naturally, but the old girl has her points. I can't complain.'

'Did you come after him?'

'Certainly not,' said Charmante, sitting down on the hall mat as though she intended to stay all night. 'I'd have thought by this time you'd have known it's the men who come after me. But as a matter of fact this time I have come after you, Lung Chung.'

'Indeed? Now isn't that sweet of you?'

'Is it?'

'I think so,' said Lung Chung in perplexity, for clearly he was not pleasing the lady.

'Then you'd better think again.'

His Highness did not answer. He wished Charmante would go away, but was too polite and too fond of her to suggest it. But if she had any tact she'd see she wasn't wanted.

'You can't have forgotten!' cried the little girl. 'Unless you never meant it.'

Lung Chung knew he had an impulsive tongue. To

what — in his first admiration — had he committed himself?

'I meant it,' he answered doggedly, for he knew he would have to keep his word.

Charmante's face lit up and she began to prance about.

'Then go and get him!'

'Do you mean George?'

'No, Teddy!'

Lung Chung ran into the study like a greyhound, seized the Teddy Bear firmly, and rushed back to Charmante. She was very pleased, saying that she hadn't expected so large an animal. She couldn't thank His Highness enough; indeed, she felt rather shy, now she had seen Teddy, about accepting the gift.

'You needn't be,' said Lung Chung. 'But don't you think you'd better go home before George comes back?'

Charmante smiled.

'I understand I'm not wanted, boy. Yet isn't it possible your problem is one that could be helped by a woman's finesse?'

Lung Chung hesitated. He guessed the meaning of the word and indeed felt he was learning quite a lot of French.

'Possibly,' he said, 'possibly.'

'Besides,' urged Charmante. 'I already know what is worrying you — I got it out of old Chink. You want to get rid of Alan and put George in his place. I've thought the matter well over, and I should quite like to have Claudia as my mistress and you for a brother.'

What a relief, on the whole, thought Lung Chung.

'Nothing warmer, dear?' he inquired, anxiously.

'No, pet. We're different breeds, and besides, I'm the fiancée of one of those pugs you pushed off the other day. I hadn't quite decided which, but now I know.'

Lung Chung gaily smiled, for he had caught a glimpse of a most lovely little Pekingese of high degree strolling down the road only that morning.

'May I congratulate you most heartily?' he said, as he had heard many people say to Claudia.

'You may kiss me if you wish. I'm too young at present, so it will be a long engagement.'

They kissed each other's noses and then sat down side by side.

'And now to business,' said Charmante. 'The idea is to make Alan show off all his bad points as quickly as possible in the hope that Claudia will take a dislike to him and break off her engagement? It shouldn't be difficult. He has a vile temper.'

'It is difficult,' sighed Lung Chung. 'She doesn't seem to mind his tempers. She's seen him in several.'

'They'll count against him in the long run. I was almost engaged myself — a private, not a public, entanglement — to the other pug you saw, but I got dog sick of his whims and jealousies. He was so much on my nerves I was compelled to break it off, or I'd have had a bad breakdown. Claudia will be the same; in these matters women are all alike, that is, good lookers . . . who can choose.'

'He's a lucky dog to win your love.'

'He is, indeed. I expect between us we shall have lots of presents. I'll let you know nearer the time what I'd like.'

Lung Chung sniffed the air appreciatively.

'Um,' he grunted. 'Love is in the air tonight, isn't it?'

'What?' snapped Charmante. 'You're not making up to me after all?'

Lung Chung used his huge eyes with good effect.

'No, little sister. But if you want to help me, I must confess that the problem of my dear mistress and Alan is no longer my sole trouble. My own worry is becoming more and more urgent every minute since I saw her this morning. Tell me, Charmante, am I too young to marry in a month or two?'

'No, I suppose not,' answered Charmante, dubiously. 'You're a dog; your bones mature more quickly than ours do, and it won't be so long before you're two years old. Why, have you seen anyone?'

Lung Chung drooped his head to hide his pink nose.

'Yes,' he confessed, shyly.

'How very funny! And does she like your scent? Who is she?'

'I don't know, but undoubtedly she is a lady of aristocratic origin. She came down the road this morning — on the leash, unfortunately — and was taken into that house on the other side of us, the big one, that's all shut up. They didn't stay long.'

'When her owners — the Everards — are at home, that's where she lives. She's a champion Peke, but

98

she's months older than you! I don't know if she'd even look at you.'

'I don't think she would; she appeared so dignified and aloof! Yet I am sure she has a most saintly nature.'

'Gosh!' cried Charmante. 'Love is decidedly in the air. She's got a jolly good opinion of herself, that one! And why do you think she has a saintly nature? She has never seemed a bit like that to me . . . always looks straight ahead in a very haughty manner.'

'The woman she was with spoke to her in a way you wouldn't speak to an ordinary dog, and she didn't utter even a grunt.'

'She must be an idiot! Our housekeeper has to watch her step with me. I must say I prefer girls with a bit of spirit.'

Lung Chung heard himself growl. He was suprised at his ferocity.

'You've got it badly, haven't you? Do tell me more!' urged Charmante.

'I haven't seen her near, and only that once. But she's white. All white. All through.'

'Tinge of yellow, I'd say!' Charmante was clearly a little jealous.

'Not a hair. Oh, I wish in a way she weren't a champion. But I could see her points were perfect.'

'There's nothing to whine about in that,' said Charmante, 'and you're not actually repulsive yourself.'

Lung Chung blushed; the pink of his nose deepened, and the artistic black bordering that had kept his breeders hopeful showed to advantage.

'If only I were more like my brother, the Flying General!'

'Bear up!' Charmante seemed to find his despair highly amusing. 'This is a democratic country, and so is modern China.'

'I wish her people would come back.'

'They are coming fairly soon, rumour has it. I suggest you go and sniff round that canine boarding establishment across the meadows. It's for ladies only, as residents, although they welcome dog visitors from time to time. I expect she's staying there.'

Lung Chung bounced up and down in his excitement.

'You really think it's possible she is so near? But they'll keep her shut up, if I know anything about kennels.'

'If I know anything about my sex, she'll manage to find a way out, if it's a case of love at first sight with both of you.'

'My darling sister!'

'If you're wise you'll keep those brotherly sentiments to yourself when my young man is about. He's the possessive sort.'

'I can understand how he feels,' sighed Lung Chung. 'It must be lovely.'

'Ugh!' grunted Charmante. 'Well, I'll say good-night. Men and dogs — you're all alike. He's got to wait, same as you.'

'Good-night, dear,' answered Lung Chung, his eyes on the hedge that separated the fields from the garden.

CHAPTER ELEVEN

Lung Chung ran across the fields, and quickly tracked out the Guest House. The doors were shut and although he could hear the sweet voices of several doubtless charming girls, there was no other sign of life. He sniffed outside for a considerable time, until a raucous voice shouted, 'Get along with you, you beast.' A window slammed. Lung Chung was not used to insults, and as it was clear that nothing could be gained by waiting, he felt it was his duty to return to Claudia. He hoped she had not missed him, for he did not wish to upset her. Luckily, she called just as he returned to the garden, and he was soon tucked up in bed, and after she had said he was 'very good' (which made him feel a terrible fraud) he received his usual bit of chocolate. An almost perfect day, he thought, as he began to dream of the beautiful little white Pekingese, his Chinese sweetheart. In the course of his dream he and Chink between them stamped out Alan completely, in the orthodox Pekingese form of fighting, not biting him with their curiously shaped mouths, but flinging their full weight upon him and not leaving him until he was incapable of moving. Dreams are convenient; it seemed as though their combined weight was more than enough to knock out and annihilate their detestable enemy.

The next morning Lung Chung was awakened by Charmante's bark below his window. He jumped on the sill, and standing on his back legs, managed to push up the catch with his front paws, and spring out to greet her.

'You are an early worm!' he cried, joyfully.

'You do say the most uncomplimentary things! First I'm a monkey, and now I'm a worm.'

Lung Chung jumped down, and licked the lady's nose to stop further complaint, but Charmante was a bit of a nagger.

'Yet you're always talking about love in a most sloppy way. I find it hard to believe you are in earnest. Of course, I am thoroughly modern myself, and so I loathe sentimentality. I don't go in for feelings.'

'Probably because, like so many people, you haven't any to boast about,' answered Lung Chung, carelessly, 'yet in my opinion, any girl, worth sniffing at, has a lot.'

'That's your view. I suppose I am entitled to my own?'

The Lion Dog gravely bowed.

'Come on, get off it, Lung Chung! Did you see her last night?'

'Alas, no. As for feeling, dear sister, don't take the conventional track. It's merely a fashion of the moment to pretend contempt for the best quality in man and beast; reaction from the false sentimentality sometimes wallowed in, in the old days. But I didn't mean to be rude. I do apologize.'

'Granted. What happened last night? I'm itching to hear.'

'The house was shut up. I couldn't get in, anywhere.'

'Bad luck! Really, one would think they were Victorian young ladies, the way they are looked after! Er — have you by any chace a surplus of bones over here this morning? Biscuits would do, if you've nothing more palatable.'

'Scarcely a surplus,' answered Lung Chung, avoiding his sister's glance.

'One or two to spare, then! You're not greedy, like old Chink, and I could do with a bit of a gnaw before breakfast. The spring has given me an appetite.'

'There may be a few at the end of the garden, but they're all well dug in.'

Charmante was not to be put off the scent. 'That's good news! Let's dig 'em out! You lead the way.'

'Ladies first!' gallantly barked the Lion Dog.

They pranced down the paths. Charmante, after nosing around, dug up several which she discarded. She was not tidy by instinct, and left them lying in the open. At last she unearthed Lung Chung's best bone, and began to gnaw it with gusto, requisitioning it without turning a hair. Chink's good eye — with a malicious glint in it — at once showed through the slit in the fence. Lung Chung's heart missed a beat. He would have to part with yet another bit of property.

'Good morning, Honourable Sir.'

'Morning to you,' growled Chink. 'I see you have your gold-digger with you.'

'There is another bone I could let you have.'

'Thanks a lot, but I don't want any of Charmante's left-offs! Nor, as a matter of fact, do I today feel up to a bone of any kind.'

This was a most unusual statement for Chink, and Lung Chung, casting a glance at him, thought he was looking rather dim.

'Not well, sir?'

'Distinctly off colour,' admitted the old fellow.

Certainly Chink's coat wanted a good brushing.

'I am sorry! Possibly you have overdone the slimming salts in your bath?'

'If you must know, I've been awake the greater part of the night. First with cats howling and yowling outside our windows, and then with toothache.'

'Oh, I say! How appalling! I remember I had a twinge or two before I lost all my milk teeth. Oughtn't you to have the vet?'

'The hound says he's too busy to come today, and he has told Edna that if it is toothache — which, of course, it is — he can't take the responsibility of getting out one of *my* growlers without another doctor to help him. Cheek! As if he couldn't get hold of

104

'I see you have your gold-digger with you'

another man to come here, if he buzzed round a bit. He's got a nerve, don't you agree?'

'Perhaps it is a long way from the other surgery.'

'Rubbish! Berry lives next door to the Guest House, and there's another vet just down the road.'

'What! Does he live next door to the Guest House? Oh, rags and bones! Oh, Chink!'

'Don't roll your eyes like that, and purr in that objectionable pussy fashion! As if I hadn't enough to put up with, without that!' scowled the old gentleman.

His face was so swollen that Lung Chung decided to forgive his lack of breeding.

'Sorry, Chink, but SHE is staying there!'

'Do bark up! I can't hear what you're saying.'

'SHE lives there! If you only knew the pangs of love!'

'The pangs of toothache are quite enough for me. What's the excitement, any old how?'

Lung Chung sighed, and raised his luminous great eyes to the blue sky. An unsympathetic, unfeeling world. One tear forced its way over his long eyelashes, and trickled down his wrinkles. Chink noticed this, and softened.

'Of all the amorous pups! You're beginning young, I must say! I suppose this is a hint you want my help with your love affair, as well as with Claudia's?'

Lung Chung wagged his feathery tail and stood up. He looked happily at his faithful friend.

'I gather the lady is staying next door to the Berrys'? You hope that if you come with me when he overhauls my teeth, which he will have to do sooner or later, it would be easy for you to slip through the dividing hedge, as the front gate is always shut. Is that it?'

'Your intelligence, Honourable Sir, is worthy of you. If I get through the hedge from the fields in the day time, I shall be in full view of the house.'

'Um, I may not have all my teeth, but my brain is as sound as ever it was. I don't want to disappoint you, Lung Chung, but you will have to wait. The pain may die down for a time; anyway, I'm going to stick it for a bit, and see what happens.'

Lung Chung put down his tail.

'But it may become quite intolerable?'

'Don't you start being a defeatist next! I've had Edna and Gerald at me all night, as if they were the only people who wanted to sleep.'

Lung Chung kept silence. He must preserve his self-control.

'Besides,' went on Chink, 'you will have more opportunities of seeing the lady pass your own gate. I dare say I'll have to give in, in the end, and meanwhile you may see someone else with a greater appeal.'

'Never!' barked the infatuated Lung Chung.

'So you think now! Oh well, cheer up! I expect it won't be long before I have to face the music.'

The Lion Dog made one more attempt to change the old man's mind.

'But until the tooth is taken out, you won't enjoy your meals as much as you usually do.'

'Don't!' howled Chink.

Charmante looked up.

'His Highness is quite right. You won't have a dog's chance of a comfortable life until you pluck up your courage, but I don't mind . . .' She put down her bone and looked at the menacing Chink, '. . . it only means more bones for me and Lung Chung! It'll be simply grand for both of us! Au revoir, darlings! I must go back now. Ever so many thanks, brother.'

She caught up the bone expertly, and made off.

'Don't tell me I didn't warn you,' growled Chink.

'Oh well, I love her. She's welcome to have it, but I wish she were more tidy by instinct. She's given me quite a bit of work to put back my property where it was.'

'Change the places, or she'll have the lot,' advised Chink.

During the next few weeks while Edna was away the old dog fought his toothache with grim determination. Whenever Lung Chung felt Claudia could spare him, he raced across the fields on his own. Sometimes he was rewarded by a glimpse of his lady, but never did he find the front or back gate open, and now the hedge in the field had the addition of fine wire netting so that not even a mouse could have slipped through. In vain Lung Chung pressed his unfortunate nose against the netting, and tried it with his young teeth. The situation was almost maddening when he heard the charming laughter of his dear one, mingling with that of the other little girls. He fell more deeply in love with her, but nothing happened in the material world. Occasionally Mary and Claudia would remark that Lung Chung took a long time at night to do his duty, and that frequently his eyes held a sad look of longing. But they never jumped to the truth of what was exciting the little Lion Dog. Usually for Claudia's sake, and because of his extreme youth, he would be very bright and gay, so that his excitable nature and temperament were supposed to be the cause of his occasional lapses from what was deemed to be normal. And, indeed, Lung Chung had a lot to make him happy. Alan was away, and every day his mistress seemed to grow fonder of her Lion Dog. He was upset when he noticed that Alan's letters often appeared to depress Claudia; yet Chink and Charmante agreed with him that his mistress looked forward to seeing George, who somehow managed to get back to London, when Alan wrote it was quite impossible to do so. Frequently when his mistress was busy, His Highness guarded the gate, and would see the lady of his heart's desire pass down the road. Sometimes she stared at him haughtily, sometimes she seemed unaware of his presence, and once or twice he noticed a faint look of amusement. Apparently she had her share of the Pekingese sense of humour.

At last, on the very day when Edna and Alan and the cast were due to return to London, and when Claudia had arranged to meet Alan at The Ivy for lunch, Chink capitulated. Gerald, who was meeting Edna at Euston, asked Edna's sister to take him at once to Mr. Berry, saying the old boy could stand the pain no longer, and might even welcome Edna with a bite, unless he were at once attended to. Chink succeeded in putting out everyone, for Edna's sister did not want to take him, and Claudia felt she must not put off Alan. But someone would have to go with him, and this information Lung Chung was glad to bark through the fence.

'And I can come too, can't I? It'll be all right, won't it?'

'Come where?'

'To Mr. Berry's surgery! Then I can make some excuse and leave you there, and slip through the front garden hedge or in at one of the gates and get to the kennels, and find her.'

'You're not very interested in my tooth, or in the agony I shall have to endure!'

'I'm not, that is, I am, of course, in a way, but this is such an exceptional chance!'

'Um, I hope it is exceptional,' grunted Chink. 'I thought at least that Gerald would take me, and see fair play. I'm not going with just anyone.'

Lung Chung almost danced in his anxiety.

'Perhaps Mary will take you, they are going to ask her. Oh, do have mercy,' he implored. 'How can it be managed for me to see my sweetheart?'

'That's easy . . . if we go — I repeat if we go! Haven't I taught you how to act . . . by the way, it won't be long now before you'll be well kicked by Alan, do you realise that? Take some of the stuffing out of you! Well, you have only to pretend you have toothache, too. Get a small bone between your gum and the side of your cheek, look miserable, refuse your breakfast, and they will be almost as fussy about you as they are about me.'

'You are clever, Chink!'

'Stale news. I've always been superior to most dogs.'

'Yes, indeed. Oh, but I say, Chink, it means being a deceiver! I don't like the idea.'

'We have to do a lot of things in this world we don't like,' said the philosopher. 'Life isn't all bones and biscuits. You don't imagine I like losing a tooth, do you? It isn't as if I could spare it easily. Now get along with you, and look snappy!'

Lung Chung wagged his tail, and went with it — drooping — into the house. He was by nature an honest pup. But he had heard it said that all was fair in love and war, and this gave him consolation. His firm refusal of breakfast, his hang-dog look, and the bone between cheek and gum convinced Claudia and Mary that there something very wrong. She rang up Gerald.

'Tummy trouble, I expect,' said Gerald cheerfully. 'Of course you mustn't disappoint Alan. Let Mary take him with Chink to Mr. Berry as you're worried. Thank Mary for me, won't you? I was at my wit's end! Our poor old chap is wretched, and in the vilest temper. I'm sorry for Berry when he gets there.'

Chink followed Mary stiffly across the fields, but Lung Chung could not subdue his high spirits. He ran backwards and forwards, and, unseen by Mary, managed to drop the bone. But he entered the surgery with his usual air of dignity and oriental calm, leaving childish things behind, and forgetting he ought to malinger. Mr. Berry and his assistant duly overhauled him and passed him as sound in every limb;

111

thoroughly healthy in mind and body, and the best tempered Peke they had ever handled. At this Chink growled furiously, and Lung Chung retired tactfully beneath a table near to the door. Immediately it was opened he darted through and out of the house. He was glad to get away from Chink's strident yells, and Mary's shriek of, 'Come back, Lung Chung!'

The hedge dividing the front gardens had no wire netting, and Lung Chung wriggled through the under-growth without difficulty. His heart stood still. There on the lawn, sniffing a daisy, was his Lovely! He coughed nervously, and she looked round, raised her proud head, shivered, and stiffened her neck. Never had Lung Chung seen such regal dignity; never had he seen one of his own Race so perfectly proportioned, so entirely all a lady of ancient lineage should be. She was staring at him in amazement.

'What do you want here, sir?' she demanded, with extreme hauteur.

'You,' answered Lung Chung, simply.

He rolled on his back, and beat the air with his paws.

CHAPTER TWELVE

'This is a select establishment for young ladies. We are carefully guarded,' said a gentle, cultured voice.

Lung Chung rose, and although he held himself proudly, he slightly lowered his head in an attempt to hide his Dudley nose. This attitude was in keeping with his facial expression of humble and tense admiration. Yet he did not wear a hang-dog look. He knew his revered ancestors would not wish him to lick the dust.

'I know it is an exclusive abode,' he managed to answer, 'although I feel it is not good enough to house so beautiful a lady.'

'We prefer our own home; our people are returning shortly from abroad, and then we shall have all our own things about us — our household gods, you know. Have you any?'

'I expect so,' answered Lung Chung, evasively, for

he did not know what the lady meant. He had, of course, Claudia, but he had discovered from Charmante that females were sometimes apt to be a little jealous.

'We think, sir, we have noticed you standing at your gate.'

Lung Chung tumbled to the use of the royal plural. His parents had often used it, and had encouraged Fei Chiang-chuan to follow suit. But the colour of his own nose had struck them as denoting a possible future tendency in his nature to the left, so this part of Lung Chung's training had been omitted. Overcome by shyness, the little Lion Dog nodded his proud head, lifted his upper lip, and showed his attractive tooth.

'We like your smile,' the lady condescended, 'and your voice is melodious to our ears. What is your honourable name?'

'Lung Chung, Your Majesty.'

'A Prince of Royal Blood — a dragon's seed! We are scarcely a majesty in these days, and when a Pekingese is admitted to our friendship, we do not use the royal plural. I shall not continue to use it with you; for you, my Prince, doubtless realise we have but a nominal right to it.'

Lung Chung waved an appreciative tail. The lady went on:

'But I am a Club Champion, Champion Kwei. My dear mother Pai Yün, is also an aristocrat of a leading kennel, and my father is Yin Yang, whose fame is probably known to you.'

She paused expectantly, panting slightly with

114

subdued pride, her tongue protruding slightly. Lung Chung bowed.

'Wonderful names . . . they mean so much,' he murmured. 'My sire is Kung, the Duke, and my mother was Chu, a pearl among women. My poor father has never got over her loss, and has remained faithful to her memory.'

'An admirable husband.'

'Yes. I can understand it, I should be just the same,' said Lung Chung. 'Perhaps I had better add that my grandparents and great grandparents and, indeed, all my ancestors, were without a blemish. How it happened,' sighed the honest little Lion, 'nobody can understand.'

'Yet I have known similar instances in aristocratic or Royal families, and although I may conventionally be mistaken, what breeders and judges might consider a blemish, makes a distinct appeal to me. It may be the dark edging all round the pink that is so charming and unique.'

'Some people have liked it, but I am not a show dog, I'm afraid.'

'That may be, but you have a noble brow, Your Highness; a distinguished bearing, and a certain decisiveness of chin that pleases me well.'

Lung Chung was speechless with joy.

'We were afraid you might not be attractive at closer range, when we — that is, I — observed your friendship with Mr. Chink, undoubtedly one of the Proletariat.'

'Chink is a great character,' said Lung Chung, stoutly.

'He has a chrysanthemum tail.'

'An accident of birth.'

'Perhaps. Does he claim pure descent?'

'Indeed, he is most keen on it, and very sniffy about almost all other dogs!'

'They always are,' observed the lady, who obviously had great knowledge of the world. 'On what does he base his pretensions?'

'He says he is an — er — an Oldberry.'

Champion Kwei tossed her Lion mane.

'Never heard of the family; however, as you have honoured him with your friendship, we may admit him later to our presence.'

The lady frisked round the lawn, and returned to the little gentleman, who courteously waited for permission to move. They were about the same size, he noticed.

'You seem . . . possible,' she smiled. 'Do you belong to the Peking Palace Association? If you are a Member we think we could dispense with further formalities.'

Lung Chung made a sound which he hoped would be mistaken for an answer in the affirmative. He felt slightly crestfallen, for he had jumped to the conclusion that the lady did not wish a ceremonial introduction, and he now lacked the moral courage to foul his pitch by admitting he had never heard of the Assocation.

Kwei looked well pleased.

'I feel we shall soon be intimate friends. Don't stand

116

on ceremony. You may call me by my pet name Wendy. I hope you will find it convenient to come again in about five weeks, after the nine o'clock news. I shall be waiting for you outside the front door. The door is not closed until ten o'clock as I have reason to believe you already know, and they mean to let me out about that time, a little later than the other guests. The people here are very fussy, I shall be thankful to get back to my own quarters. Anyway, I shall hide you well before they come along to call me in, if I am right in my surmise you would like to spend the night?'

'Spend the night!' repeated Lung Chung. 'Oh, Wendy darling, could you name the day?' and in his excitement he began to dance round his own dear little Champion, who sat back and laughed softly at his antics. At the conclusion he stood up on his back legs, and smiling, placed his left paw on his heart.

'The fifteenth of next month, dearest. I feel I have chosen well, and without any interference from the foreign powers, friendly though they are, to China. And I consider you a great improvement on their choice, Fei Chiang-chuan. He was well enough in his way, and of good family, but he had no sense of humour.'

Lung Chung's mouth dropped open in astonishment. Kwei nodded.

'The breeders here consider we are engaged to be married. They wrote to my master and mistress and said they had fixed up everything. Apparently it was agreed the match was suitable. Really, these humans — even the best of them — sometimes take a bit too much upon themselves, don't you agree? They never consulted me, and after all I am the chief person concerned! Certainly they brought over the young gentleman for my inspection, but they failed to notice that I at once turned my back on him, and I admit he did not seem drawn to me.'

'The Flying General has always declared he would remain a bachelor!'

'I have heard that story before, anyway, he will fulfil his ambition as far as I am concerned. But what do you know about Fei Chiang-chuan?'

'He is my dear brother, my twin.'

'So we were not mistaken. We felt we should not be making a misalliance. How nature and instinct combine, if one is in possession of all one's faculties! As your brother was considered good enough, no question can be raised about you.'

'You think not?'

'I know. One of our family might inherit 'it' but even if that were the case, that is the child I should favour. I should love them all, of course, with the greatest ardour.'

Wendy shook her thick coat, and kicked up the lawn with her dainty back legs. Lung Chung followed her example. In the distance the gardener viewed this combined action with animosity.

'Tell me, dear Wendy,' said the little Lion Dog, 'have you an ambition, too?'

Wendy stood still and closed her lovely eyes. 'Yes,

but it does not resemble your brother's. It is very different. It is to be a mother, my sweet Lung Chung.'

'Kwei darling, how alike we are! Mine is to become a father.'

'You may lick my face, Lion Dog, and then you must go. I see our gardener coming, and he is very proud of this lawn.'

After their embrace, Champion Kwei ran back to her dwelling, and disappeared from sight. But Lung Chung stood in a dream of happiness, looking at the grass she had kicked up so cleverly. The sun broke out, and he felt himself to be at one with it, and Wendy and all creation. Even with the gardener, who was approaching with unseemly rapidity. The scents were more beautiful; the green of the rest of the lawn was more vivid, the pattern of the leaves above held more meaning, as did life itself, to the enchanted little dog. But soon the gardener's howl of wrath, Chink's yells, and Mary's alarmed cries, 'Lung Chung! Lung Chung! Where are you?' brought the ardent lover back to earth.

'Oh, where *is* Lung Chung?' moaned Mary.

'Yes, where is the little beast? I want to get home!' yapped Chink.

Poor old man! He was greatly to be pitied. He had never in the whole of his long life had a single love affair, or if he had had, he had kept it very dark. Quietly Lung Chung slipped through the undergrowth.

'Oh, there you are, precious! Come along, come along!' cried Mary.

Lung Chung could not help congratulating himself on his appeal to the ladies. He rushed across to Mary, not bothering to conceal his high spirits.

'Why, he seems quite mad about you!' said Mr. Berry.

'Dogs always know the people who like them, don't they?' answered Mary. 'At least, that's what I always say.'

CHAPTER THIRTEEN

Chink sounded in a worse temper than usual, and was trying Mary's patience to the utmost. He now turned his attention to Lung Chung.

'Of all the inconsiderate pups!' he snarled. 'We've been hanging about in this east wind for hours; how I hate it — it always finds out my weak points. And I don't want to catch cold in my gums next, I can tell you.'

'Oh, you won't,' purred Lung Chung. 'The sun is divine.'

'Don't irritate me with your inane remarks, they make me dog tired of you! Who do you think you are? The lady has received your advances graciously, has she? Then take my advice; drop her as you would drop an unpleasant bone, and bury the memory of her. All women, with the exception of Edna and

Claudia — and they're humans, remember — are false and fickle.'

'I can't agree with you!' Lung Chung wanted to bark back a stronger observation, but he exercised his self-control. The old boy did look distinctly under the weather.

'I didn't expect you would. But love is an illness — a disease. Thank goodness I'm immune from it. Age has its compensations, even if it deprives one of one's teeth.'

'Did it hurt much?'

'Don't ask absurd questions. Do two extractions with abscesses on the roots of both teeth usually hurt? I wish you would try and develop a modicum of common sense.'

'Sorry,' apologized Lung Chung.

'So I should think,' growled Chink.

Although hope of a glorious future lay ahead, the next few weeks dragged. Chink, with swollen cheeks, remained immersed in gloomy self-pity; Charmante was distrait and spent most of her time peering round the corner of her gate, waiting for her pug. She went for walks across the heath with him, never once suggesting that Lung Chung should make a third. Alan was constantly in the house, and although he often made Claudia and himself unhappy, he yet stood over her like a dog with a bone he doesn't care for himself, but is determined not to relinquish to any other dog. George wanted Claudia, and Alan knew this as well as Lung Chung. If ever there was a dog-in-the-manger it was the detestable, conceited actor.

Lung Chung almost hated him. Before his own marriage to Champion Kwei took place, he must somehow get rid of Alan and put George in his place.

At last Chink announced his wounds were healed and that he and Edna, with Claudia and Lung Chung, were going that afternoon to the rehearsal as the play was soon to be produced. He said firmly that the time had now come for Lung Chung to do his part. Charmante, who had dug out the last of her friend's bones, carried it across.

'How are things going, darling?' asked Lung Chung, trying to rouse himself to take a brotherly interest in Charmante's affair and so momentarily to forget the task that lay ahead.

'We have had one or two tiffs, but I've got him practically to heel. And how is your sweetheart? Is she licking you well into shape?'

'I would fulfil her least desire.'

'An ideal husband. Obviously you can't call your soul your own, but personally I prefer more pugnacity in a dog.'

'The infatuation won't last,' sneered Chink.

'How do you know?' asked Charmante, rudely. 'You've never been married.'

'Nor have you!'

'No, but I'm going to be.'

'Poor chap.'

Charmante tossed her head.

'It's lucky for you he isn't here! He's young! He could more than stand up to you in defence of me.'

123

'When I was young,' growled Chink, 'little girls were seen and not heard.'

'Modern little girls aren't like that.'

Lung Chung frowned. He hated to hear his friends snarling at one another.

'What time do we start?' he asked.

Chink said the car would call immediately after lunch, and that he hoped Lung Chung would be ready and not keep people waiting. Charmante put a paw on the Lion Dog's feathery arm.

'You will take care of yourself, won't you? I consider it is highly dangerous to try and trip up Alan. It's all very well for Chink, at your expense, to plan liberation for Claudia, but a woman of spirit ought not lean on another animal. She ought to face up to it that Alan's a dirty dog.'

Lung Chung answered that, when in love, what people and dogs ought to do and what they do were seldom compatible. Chink again stated his conviction that love was a mental illness, and anyway Lung Chung had taken on the job and it must now not be dodged.

'I don't see why Chink couldn't have offered himself as a football,' Charmante observed, as she accompanied Lung Chung back to his house, 'he seems as keen on the idea as he is on that bone of yours he's just found and is standing over. He knew I wanted it, but I didn't think it was worth another scrap.'

'I wish you and Chink were more friendly,' said

Lung Chung, who was feeling distinctly sloppy this morning.

'Oh, he's not bad as old dogs go,' Charmante answered. 'I don't really object to him; he has his points. All the same, he could well be spared by many people, whereas you are young. It would be sad if you were cut off prematurely. Well, au revoir; I hope you won't get badly hurt or, at the worst, escape with your life.' Her round eyes looked distinctly damp.

'Au revoir,' repeated Lung Chung, and watched his sister run away with tears not far from his own eyes. Yes, it would be sad, for his life had scarcely begun.

That afternoon Claudia greeted Alan rather stiffly.

'Alan's looking like a bear,' grunted Chink. 'I shall keep well out of his way, for I don't feel sufficiently fit to give him a nip.'

'I wish I could keep out of his way.'

'Surely after all this time and the trouble I've taken with you, you are not going to funk it?'

'I'm as good as my bark, I hope. The rehearsal isn't going too well, is it? The producer doesn't seem to like Alan's performance. The fact he's already in a nasty temper won't make it easier for me.'

'You'd better get ready,' answered Chink, without the least show of sympathy. 'They are going to take your scene next. You run into the fray at the words "Do you think you can ever care for me?" As if June could ask such a fool's question; utter tosh! Anyway, don't miss your cue.'

Lung Chung took a deep breath. He stood all square; his expression was inscrutable as he eyed the performers; his dignity was unshaken, and he knew now he would put up a good show. What he did not know was whether he would survive, for Alan was a heavy man, and to run in between his legs and attempt to throw him down was a big risk. He had not long to wait, and at the given words he ran in. He never knew exactly what happened; he heard Claudia call out and Edna scream, but before Alan fell Lung Chung found himself hurtling through the air, a mere lump of pain. He crashed on the hard floor. And there his activity ceased. He had no need to pretend to faint, for with a groan — that went to the seasoned heart of Chink — he passed out.

When he recovered consciousness, he knew he had succeeded as a Realist. He lay still with shut eyes, but Claudia's voice, low and passionate, was saying:

'Alan, I'll never forgive you for this! A man who can kick a small dog — or any dog — is a cur!'

Alan was dusting his trousers with his white, well-kept hands. Lung Chung watched him through his long lashes.

'I didn't mean to hurt him badly, but the brute got deliberately in between my legs — deliberately, I tell you!'

With difficulty the little Chinese gentleman refrained from showing his small tooth. Then he noticed that Claudia was taking off her ring.

'Nonsense! You are always accusing Lung Chung or Chink of annoying you. I'm tired of you! Clearly we could never live together.'

Alan went pale. His pride was hurt; nothing else.

'So it's a case of "Love me, love my dog," is it? Well, I for one would never take a back seat.'

'That's obvious! Please go away. Here is the vet Edna sent for.'

Lung Chung discreetly closed his eyes. He kept them shut while Mr. Berry felt him all over and kept a stethoscope on his chest for a considerable time.

'Surely I am very ill,' thought Lung Chung. 'How pretty I must look lying here. I wish Wendy could see me. How sorry she would be for me. Supposing I were to die?'

But the verdict was a cheerful one.

'He's a highly strung little chap. A few bruises; nothing to speak of. He's thinking too much of his symptoms at present, but he'll soon be himself again. They are a most courageous race. Keep him quiet, and give him a light diet.'

'But he hasn't opened his eyes yet!'

'He was looking at you when I came in.'

Claudia knelt down and took Lung Chung's head on her lap. Oh, moment of bliss! Oh, if only Wendy could see how greatly his mistress valued her Lion Dog. Chink was making derisive noises in the background.

'I must say, Lung Chung, you quite took me in,' he chuckled, 'I had no idea you had so much talent. You'd make your fortune at Hollywood, I believe, in spite of — er — of IT.'

'Are you quite sure his heart is sound?' Claudia was asking.

'Quite! What a little beauty he is. *And* knows it! He's

127

almost as perfect as Champion Kwei; her owners live next door to you in Hampstead.'

'Yes, they are away just now; Kwei is a lovely little creature. When are the Everards returning?'

'Very soon, I believe. Oh, Mrs. Williams, as I'm here, would you like me to examine poor old Chink? If he's still below par, I can give him an injection here and now.'

'Yes, do! Thanks so much, Mr. Berry,' said Edna.

No needles for me then, thought Lung Chung, and his spirits revived at once. He smiled sympathetically at Chink. The old man was for it. But not at all. Chink growled ferociously and backed, showing his great open spaces.

'Very well, angel,' agreed Edna, at once. 'You see, Mr. Berry, he's been so upset about our dear Lung Chung. The tears have been pouring down his cheeks; it's nerves this time, not bad temper. As he is in such a state of agitation, I feel an injection would scarcely be wise, do you? We've all been frightened to death; the whole dreadful affair was so utterly unexpected.'

Mr. Berry hastily and enthusiastically agreed. He at once departed. Chink burst out laughing and rolled about from side to side. Although Lung Chung still felt dizzy and peculiar, a sound broke from his black lips that was like an echo of his usual laughter. Claudia mistook it for a groan and lifted him carefully from the floor.

'My poor innocent darling,' she murmured. 'How could Alan be so cruel?'

'I like that!' Chink guffawed. 'You have certainly

done credit to my training. 'Pon my word, Lung Chung, I believe you'd get away with anything.'

CHAPTER FOURTEEN

The next day, when Claudia went out, Chink came to bear the invalid company. Charmante had accompanied him, but Mary had turned her away saying, 'One at a time and no more, my dear.' Charmante had left her Teddy Bear behind on the step, and Lung Chung was anxious to have it returned to her. Mary simply would not understand.

'O.K.,' said Chink, 'I'll take it back and tell her you have more toys than you know what to do with.'

Lung Chung glanced at his collection.

'I have a lot,' he admitted, 'but The Lady Champion Kwei may like one or two.'

'Clever little boy,' grinned Chink. 'Over the fields and far away, I don't think. You haven't lost much time, have you?'

'I must be quite well in a week! We — er — we are getting married on the fifteenth of the month.'

'There's more in you than meets the eye,' said Chink. 'I suppose you chose that date because, as it's the first night of the play, we'll all be so worked up that even Claudia and Mary won't miss you.'

'The Lady Kwei chose the date, I left it entirely to her.'

'A fortunate coincidence, if you really are going through with the affair.'

'You don't seem to understand I am deeply in love.'

'I only hope it may last! Well, how are you feeling after what happened yesterday?'

'Tired, and in some pain when I move.'

'Stiffness,' commented the old man. 'You wait until you're my age and have sciatica. Then you'll know what pain is. What did you have for lunch today?'

'Boiled chicken and rice.'

'My word, you're doing yourself well! A slice of sirloin and celery last night. Guess what the new cook had the impertinence to offer me! Horseflesh! Of course I wouldn't touch it.'

'What did you have?'

'Edna's cutlets. I will say one thing for the woman, she can cook. And now I've shown her where she gets off, I had quite a decent luncheon and two bones.'

'Two!'

'Yes, but I've shoved one through the fence for you. You'd better hurry up and get well before Charmante or the gardener finds it.'

'It's most generous of you, Chink.'

'Pray don't mention it,' Chink stood up, stretched, and sat down again. 'With my sciatica I find it well not to sit in one position for too long. Well, things are progressing, aren't they? You've heard the engagement is broken off.'

'You forget I was there at the time. But Claudia looks so sad, Chink. I rather wonder if we ought to have interfered.'

'I like that, after all my trouble! Get a bone and gnaw it,' said Chink, rudely. 'Organisation isn't easy, I can tell you! It took a lot of time and trouble to arrange our plot.'

'Organisation? That means thinking out work for other people to do, doesn't it? I'd rather like to be an organiser,' observed Lung Chung, licking his biggest bruise.

He was told not to be cheeky, and feeling weak, tears came into the eyes of the invalid.

'My life was jeopardized in the cause.'

'Possibly. But I think we may feel that our intervention will have good results. Claudia is a sensible woman and has, I am convinced, a good idea of George's sound points. It may take a few months to bring them together, but another crisis would do the trick, or my name's not Chink Oldberry.'

'I don't feel strong enough to offer myself again, relying on my brute force. I might not recover from a second injury, and I have Champion Kwei to consider.'

Chink said that he had had enough hard work to last him for some time, and suggested they should now take a little nap. They slept soundly the whole afternoon, and did not wake until Gerald Williams was shown into the room.

'Oh, so this is where you are, Chink, you rascal! I was getting quite worried about you. Edna's on her way home, and is coming here first, so we can stop until she arrives. And how are you, Lung Chung? Feeling better, little fellow?'

'Yes, thanks,' murmured His Highness, wagging his tail and giving Gerald a quick lick.

'Now then, now then!' snapped Chink. 'No trespassing, even if you aren't too fit. You are a spoilt pup!'

'I'm afraid I am. Do you know, I find Gerald is a very reliable sort of man — like George. He is the type of human I instinctively trust.'

'Oh, rather! That's why we keep him about the place.'

The telephone bell rang. After answering it in the hall, Gerald returned and took up a newspaper. He seemed suddenly to be in excellent spirits.

'Yes, it's often well to let sleeping dogs lie,' remarked Chink. 'While we were nodding this afternoon, Lung Chung, I have a feeling that another crisis occurred that has not displeased Gerald. I say, do you remember where I hid my biscuit the last time I came? I am positive I didn't eat them all! I could have sworn I put one under this rug.'

'Our carpets and rugs are swept every day. Yes, you left one there, but Mary found it and gave it to me.'

'And you wolfed it? I never did!'

'That's just too bad,' smiled Lung Chung. He put a

delicate paw under his cushion and threw the biscuit towards Chink.

'I knew it was your property.'

'Thanks very much.' Chink began to crunch his treasure, then stopped. 'Listen! I hear them coming. I must welcome them at the front door.'

He trotted quickly after Gerald. Lung Chung pricked his ears and stood up. Yes, Claudia and Edna had arrived. His Highness knew he ought to stay in his basket, but he needed all his self-control to stay where he was. After animated talk in the hall, Edna, followed by Claudia and Gerald, came into the room. The organiser, looking very pleased with himself, brought up the rear. He nodded happily across.

'I'm right as usual. There has been a crisis. Alan's walked out on them.'

'His name will be mud in the profession! Have you ever known an actor of repute do such a thing?' stormed Edna.

'No, my dear, but if it's any satisfaction to you, he's let himself in for heavy damages,' answered Gerald, calmly, showing his business ability in what, Lung Chung considered, was a masterly manner.

'It isn't as though George hasn't had to play the part again and again in the last few weeks. And the play is a good one, *not* written specially for Alan,' said Claudia.

'Yes, it will give George his chance. I am glad of that, and I like acting with him. Except for the fact that Alan has sprung a last minute surprise on the lot

134

of us, which means intensive rehearsing, especially for George and me, I wouldn't care.'

Gerald offered Edna a cigarette and filled his pipe. Claudia took up her Lion Dog, and for once he allowed her to nurse him. She didn't smoke like the others, and he knew he was, at the moment, her consolation. Later on, this duty would be performed by George. Lung Chung liked to be petted and praised, but he drew the line as a rule at being — or rather acting the part of — a lap dog, even Claudia's, now that he was grown up and engaged to be married.

'And merely because he was offered a film contract! I have known men with a tenth of Alan's income lose any amount of money rather than let down a play,' went on Edna.

'But don't you think it may work out for the best?' asked Claudia. 'George has had to take his place so often in the provinces. You said the managers seemed to like him.'

'In my opinion he will put up a much better show,' said Gerald, satisfactorily. 'And there's time for several rehearsals before the first night.'

'And my first night, too,' thought Lung Chung, dreamily. 'I hope dear Kwei won't forget to call me in.'

The garden gate clicked. His Highness jumped down carefully and ran as fast as his bruised limbs would allow him to welcome George in the hall.

'Come in quickly!' he barked. 'Make hay while the sun shines. It's up to you now, George, to carry on. Chink and I have done our best for you.'

George at once understood. He picked up the emotional Lung Chung, gently tucked him under one arm and went at once into the room. He put the little gentleman down to guard his mistress, who smiled at both of them.

'I shall do my best for the play, Edna. I've had to put in a good deal of work on it already. It isn't as if I haven't played the part fairly often. The first night will be trying for all of us, but somehow I feel things will work out well in the long run.'

'Of course they will,' assented Edna. 'It's only I hate the idea of his getting away with everything.'

'He won't,' smiled George. 'In fact, he hasn't, has he?'

George's eyes were on Claudia.

'He certainly hasn't,' agreed Gerald.

Chink coughed.

'And as I shall be in Edna's dressing room, he will not get any of our property. I suppose you intend to be out on the loose that night, Lung Chung?'

'I should not describe it like that, but have it your way, Chink. Anyway, I don't believe Claudia will want me; all her attention will be given to George.'

'Let us hope he doesn't let us down next,' said Chink. 'If the play's a failure Edna will have something to growl about.'

'He won't,' answered Lung Chung. 'George will soon have every incentive to show all his points.'

'What are you yapping about? What incentive except to make a name for himself?'

'And a name for her! I tell you, Chink, my sweet mistress will be engaged before the first night.'

Chink showed his teeth.

'You're tellin' me, you young dog, you! But you may be right. George is out to make a dead set at her, now Alan's off the scent.'

CHAPTER FIFTEEN

It was early evening of the First Night. Chink, a hang-dog look on his usually inscrutable countenance, a red ribbon tied securely round his middle-age spread, was hunched against the gap in the fence. His two friends peeped at him: both were well groomed. Charmante had a royal blue ribbon fastened on her leather collar; and Mary had decked Lung Chung out in a white bow, little knowing how appropriate was the choice. In view of his supposed delicate state of health, it had been decided to leave him at home, but the ribbon had been presented to him, in case he felt jealous. How little Mary or anyone knew how he was feeling; Charmante had an idea, but Chink pretended he had forgotten all about Champion Kwei.

'Can we come over to you?' barked Lung Chung. 'We've such good news! You'll never guess, will he, Charmante?'

'Not he! Mon Dieu, Chink! How smart you look. I'd sell my soul for that red ribbon.'

'If you had one.'

'You are a polite old gentleman, I must say!'

'Don't scrap, please, tonight of all nights. Anything wrong, old boy?'

'Everything. Just my luck. Liver. Kidneys. Stomach. All my intestines, and dinner will be in half an hour.'

'Oh, give it a miss for once,' advised His Highness. 'Teeth all wrong, too, I suppose?'

'No,' snarled Chink. 'Why should they be? I'm merely as sick as a dog. It's those filthy slimming salts.'

'My ancestors! Did you take them internally? I say, Chink, really at your age you should know better.'

'It's easy to be wise after the event. I've tried them out in my bath for ages, and they didn't do the slightest good. It's too bad. I wanted to look my best tonight. Edna's in her usual first-night temperamental state, and wouldn't listen when I growled the ribbon was too tight. What with one thing and another, I live a dog's life.'

'But even I knew your slimming salts were for the bath, although I don't use them myself; not necessary in my case,' observed Charmante, rolling her eyes in astonishment.

'You puffed up puppy.'

'I believe,' said Charmante to Lung Chung, 'that we could between us get that ribbon off. You could take one end and I'll have the other, and then pull in opposite directions. That might give him some relief. It wouldn't be difficult; it's a single knot.'

'It's a mistake to show off your waistline'

'And then, perhaps, he'd give you the ribbon,' whispered Lung Chung.

'Wait a bit,' panted Chink. 'No tricks at the moment.'

'You can't be sick here,' cried Lung Chung, in alarm. He didn't want Charmante to be ill; puppies are so easily sick.

'Can't I?' groaned Chink; and was.

They moved nearer to the rose garden, and waited silently until Chink indicated he felt slightly better. Would it really be possible, he inquired quite civilly, to take off the ribbon that was gripping him in a vice?

'We can, if I may wear it afterwards,' said Charmante, with a woman's true instinct for a bargain. 'It's a mistake to show off your waistline, but it's a different kettle of fish with me. Or would you like to take it to the Lady Kwei, Lung Chung?'

'No, thanks, darling, but let's be quick. Then we can tell him the news.'

With the zest of youth they seized the ends of the ribbon, and tugged and shook it with so much vigour they nearly pulled the old dog over. They paid no attention to his growls and Charmante, mounting on his body, explored the knot with her teeth.

'I see now how it goes.'

Once again they seized the ends, and skipping and dancing, they lengthened their retreat; finally Lung Chung let go, and Charmante ran off with her prize.

'Come and have a tug of war.'

Lung Chung could not resist chasing her, and they had a grand game. They were out of breath when

141

they returned to the invalid, Charmante dangling the ribbon over her wrist.

'If you feel better, could you help me to tie your girdle round Charmante? She's so keen to have a sash, and she'd look,' the Lion Dog took a deep breath, 'most charmante, don't you agree?'

'Practising flattery for later on in the evening, I take it? Well, I don't mind giving you a hand.'

When the ribbon was secured round the young lady, she walked across to the lily pond to have a look at herself.

'A conceited puss,' grunted Chink. 'How's Claudia? These First Nights are trying to all concerned.'

'She's as sweet as usual, just as if . . . but wait until Charmante comes back before I tell you. How is Edna?'

'Our place is in a turmoil, and when I showed signs of ill-health she said it was almost the last straw to break a camel's back. But then, she always talks incoherently before a London production. Nobody can please her. Not even me!'

'Not Gerald?'

'Gerald! No, he's absolutely hounded down. He says he's a safety valve. But I wouldn't put up with it, in his shoes.'

'What would you do?' asked Lung Chung. He felt he could never like Chink again if he answered he would turn on his mistress.

'I don't know,' answered Chink, evasively, 'but today she's been enough to make a saint — let alone a husband — cast her to the dogs! In my opinion, this highly-strung business is a bit overdone in the profession. Ah, here is Charmante. What's the news? I bet I know.'

'All right, clever, then tell us!'

'Claudia and George are engaged. It's not a question of guessing. Didn't I arrange the whole bag of tricks?'

'Why, of course you did!' cried Lung Chung, who was so happy he wanted the old dog to have pleasure, too.

'There's nothing like blowing your own trumpet, is there? Well, thanks for my sash, it's most becoming. I'll be seein' you, Chink, au revoir! And good luck — the very best — dear brother.'

Charmante danced away. The dinner gong sounded. Chink made for his house, walking rather sedately. Lung Chung hid in the garden. Nobody called to him. He felt a little sad when Claudia drove away with Mary. But only for a moment. He lifted his proud head, and smiled in the darkness. The time went by very pleasantly; at last Big Ben sounded from the radio of a near-by house.

Lung Chung raced across the fields, into the Berrys' garden, and as he wriggled through the undergrowth, he heard Kwei's gentle call.

* * *

'Yes, our George made a great hit,' Chink grunted. 'I always considered his talent superior to Alan's, and that he has better bone and muscle, and muzzle. Anyway, he went down very well, very well, indeed.'

'I'm glad,' murmured Lung Chung. He yawned. Chink shot his head forward. 'I beg your pardon, but I am so sleepy. I got back hours after the rest of you.'

'I heard you creeping in long after dawn, with your tail between your legs! So you got on well with the lady?'

Charmante tossed her head.

'You do state the obvious, Chink! Anyone can see Lung Chung is a lump of happiness.'

'Oh, he'll soon have his eye on someone else.'

'I am not that kind of dog,' cried Lung Chung. 'You should know that by this time, Chink.'

'And Edna made a success, too,' said the old dog, avoiding argument for once. 'I felt quite proud of her. She was a help to George.'

'I usually prefer men to women,' observed Charmante, 'but for a woman, Edna's a good sort, although some of her points are not up to Claudia's. Did you hear when the wedding is to be, Chink? I have to arrange my own plans.'

'In about three months. So Champion Kwei improves on acquaintance, does she?'

'Don't talk like that about my wife,' growled Lung Chung.

'Hoighty-toighty. All the same, you've both caused a spot of bother. The Guest House people have been round, and have given the game away to Claudia. Did you know your brother, the Flying General, had been brought over yesterday specially for your — er — wife? And they thought he was with her last night, when all the time it was you!'

'Naturally he stepped aside for me. When the Guest House people saw me, they seemed to approve of my darling's choice.'

'Because they thought that you were your brother.'

'I should not have interfered if my sweetheart had been drawn to Fei Chiang-chuan, but she assured me she could never feel more than a platonic affection for him, which is as well, for he made up his mind very early on, that he would always be a bachelor! It was a pleasant night, so he went ratting.'

'It was a good thing Gerald was with Claudia and was able to adjust the business details. He is sure Kwei's owners will pay Brown the stud fee just the same, or something of the kind.'

'The Flying General will never make a stud dog. We are an obstinate family.'

Chink pointed out how individual every Pekingese was, which provoked Charmante, who said pugs were, too, only more so. When the scrap died down, Chink, who was more accustomed to late nights than the others, and had slept coming back in the car, said Mr. Brown was probably furious, all the same, with Lung Chung for poking his nose — and what a nose — into his business arrangements. But His Highness did not resent Chink's attempt at an insult; he was in love and at peace with the world.

The intervening time passed quickly for Lung Chung, until the day came when Kwei did not run across the fields with the other guests, and meet her husband — meetings the Guest House people had sensibly allowed. Her friends said she was well, but would not be about again for a while.

Lung Chung accepted the situation which was not unexpected. Wendy was to have her wish granted;

and he would be allowed to see his little ones sooner than most fathers. The preparations began for Claudia's wedding to George, and Lung Chung was rather worried about his wedding present. Then he heard that he had become the father of three handsome boys and a little girl. Kwei and the family took up residence in her own home, and there Lung Chung was allowed to visit her. The children pulled Kwei's beautiful heart-shaped ears and she seemed to enjoy it, but when they attacked Lung Chung's, he gravely but firmly forbade this form of play. He and Kwei talked over the future of their offspring, three of whom showed every sign of becoming champions of the future.

'I feel that before your dear mistress marries, I ought to call and show her the children,' said Kwei one day. 'My people are going to see her this afternoon; would you like us to come along, too, dear husband?'

'Indeed, I would! Claudia is longing to see the little ones. I've been wondering, dear Kwei, if you and I could offer her a wedding present?'

'Of what?' smiled Kwei, who was undoubtedly gifted with the mind-reading common to the Pekingese.

'You know, sweetheart. And I would love to have one of them with me. I wonder which Claudia would choose?'

'I think I know,' smiled Wendy, fondly. 'Well, I'll bring them along just after tea. See that the doors are open for us.'

Lung Chung spent an anxious afternoon. Mr. and

Mrs. Everard seemed to think he was not only lovely, but an amusing little dog. They did not realise how seriously His Highness took his duties as a father. At last he pricked his ears, as the familiar patter came across the hall, and into the room walked Kwei, followed by the children.

'Oh, the darlings!' cried Claudia, enraptured. 'Oh, aren't they like their parents?'

Kwei bowed; Lung Chung helped her to bring forward each puppy for a ceremonial introduction.

'Our eldest Yin Yin.'

'Our second son, Hsiao.'

'Our daughter, Hwa Pei.'

'Our youngest son, Ling Ling.'

'You must have one of them,' said Mrs. Everard. 'We insist.'

'But they will surely all be champions! How like Hsiao is to Lung Chung, except he hasn't . . .'

Kwei pushed forward her daughter.

'But Hwa Pei has!'

'Oh yes, Petal inherits her father's most attractive feature. Then if you really want me to have one as a wedding present, may I have Hwa Pei? She is so like Lung Chung when I first saw him in the shop window.'

The parents were delighted, for Hwa Pei was their favourite. Chink poked his head round the door, and Petal ran forward and pulled his ears, first one and then the other.

'You mustn't, darling! Forgive her, Mr. Chink, if you please.'

'There is nothing to forgive, madam,' murmured Chink, highly gratified at his popularity.

'She'd better not try that on with Aunty,' said Charmante sauntering in with George. 'I must say I never expected to see Mr. Chink put up with frivolity of the sort. He was very down on me as a puppy.'

'Charmante, my sister. This is my wife, Champion Kwei.'

The ladies bowed.

'But you are only a pug, not one of us!' said Chink. 'I am a member of the Oldberry family, my lady.'

'Indeed?' said Kwei politely. 'How very nice.'

'I wonder what they're talking about. Chinese is such a difficult language to understand, don't you think?' said Claudia.

'Pugs are Chinese, too,' said George, who instinctively knew when anyone was feeling lonely or a little hurt. 'My one is full of character and will make a perfect maiden aunt, although she'll pretend to bully sometimes, just for fun.'

Charmante smiled at Champion Kwei.

'Men are great fools sometimes, aren't they? One would imagine that George is the only dog who is soon going to be mated. Maiden aunt, indeed!'

Lung Chung left his wife's side for a brief moment, and kissed his sister's smiling mouth.

'I wish you all happiness.'

He went back to Champion Kwei, and pushed Ling Ling away from his mother's side. Ling Ling squealed.

'Don't be rough with him,' said Kwei, nervously. 'He can't help being agile. I know he's rather selfish

148

'What a comfort you are to me!'

at the moment and has a lot of puppy fat, but he isn't terribly strong.'

'He must be taught self-control,' answered Lung Chung, taking up his former position. 'And respect for both of us.'

'All the little ones feel that,' said Kwei, fondly. 'May I only trust, my dear sister-in-law, that your happiness will soon equal ours?'

'Thanks very much,' said Charmante, with simulated modern callousness.

Yin Yin, the silver seal, was pulling Chink's ears; Petal was tugging at his tail. The old man was bearing up wonderfully.

'Would you like to give me a kiss, Hwa Pei?'

Petal dropped his tail and lifted her Dudley nose. They kissed. Claudia caught her up. Kwei watched her daughter anxiously, while Claudia and George, and her own people, all admired the bright child.

'I think, Lung Chung, as Petal grows up it will be necessary to keep an eye on her. She's going to be a very attractive girl.'

'Undoubtedly. But with you and Claudia and all of us as watch dogs, there's little reason to fear she will run astray.'

Champion Kwei looked at Lung Chung with deep affection.

'What a comfort you are to me!' she gently sighed. 'My children have a father in a thousand. I do not wonder your mistress adores you.'

Lung Chung lifted his upper lip, and showed his tooth.

'And they have a mother in a thousand, too, Wendy my pet. How lucky I am to have your love and Claudia's, in spite of my Dudley nose! And it hasn't even interfered with my career, for I never wanted to be a show dog.'

The puppies stopped playing, and solemnly regarded their parents, Petal with her head well up.

'I love your nose,' said Kwei, fondly.

'And so do we, Daddy!' squeaked the offspring.